DELPHA GREEN & COMPANY

DELPHA GREEN & COMPANY

Vera and Bill Cleaver

J. B. LIPPINCOTT COMPANY

PHILADELPHIA AND NEW YORK

U.S. Library of Congress Cataloging in Publication Data

Cleaver, Vera.
 Delpha Green & company.
  SUMMARY: With the help of his thirteen-year-old daughter, a
man who qualified for the ministry while serving a prison term
founds an independent church that introduces hope to an apathetic,
resigned community.
  [1. Social problems—Fiction] I. Cleaver, Bill, joint author. II. Title.

PZ7.C57926De   [Fic]   79-172141
ISBN-0-397-31236-9 (pbk.)   ISBN-0-397-31344-6 (lib. bdg.)

U.S. 1658649

DELPHA
GREEN &
COMPANY

AQUARIUS
THE WATER BEARER
JANUARY 21ST THROUGH
FEBRUARY 19TH

Lost in tomorrow within
The midnight rainbow of Uranus.

ONE

One day when I was twelve it was made known to me that a childless, schoolteacher couple had desires for me to go and live with them. Their name was Sistrunk and they were odd. I do like odd people; they are interesting.

In my first meeting with these people I tied my long hair under my chin, which is a little nervous habit I have, and said, "You shouldn't look at me so hungry now. If I go home with you it doesn't mean I can be yours forever, you know. I've got my own family and when all this mess is straightened out we're going to be together again."

"Oh, we understand that perfectly," said Mr. Sistrunk who had a really startling smile.

"You have the most beautiful hair," said Mrs. Sistrunk. "When I was your age mine was that same color. So blond it was almost white."

"What I mean to say is, I want to be very carefully honest with you," I said. "It is the way I was raised. Some people say things they don't mean. They think other people won't remember but they always do. One time I almost got myself killed for saying something I wasn't careful about. I told a girl I knew I was a high trapeze artist. Her cousin happened to be one. She was with a circus and when she came for a visit about a year later I had to pretend I knew how to dance on a wire we strung up between some trees. When the doctor got there he said at first my neck was broken but it wasn't. I was in bed for a week though."

"Lies," said Mrs. Sistrunk, "are a lot of trouble. I just can't be bothered with them." She was looking at me and holding onto Mr. Sistrunk's hand.

"I see you are wondering about my eyes so we'd better get them out of the way, too, before we go any further," I said. "They're both mine. I was just born with the right one blue and the left one green, that's all."

"I hadn't really noticed they were different colors," said Mrs. Sistrunk. "You have lovely eyelashes. They're like little white spokes."

"If they make you feel like I am hiding something from you or anything like that maybe you had better look around for a normal kid. Maybe you'd prefer my sister, Tillie. Her real name is Tallullah but everybody calls her Til-

10

lie. She's a year younger than me and we aren't anything alike. Both her eyes are the same color and you always know what she's going to say even before she says it."

"She sounds fascinating but it is really you we are interested in," said Mrs. Sistrunk.

"I also have three normal brothers," I said. "Hershal, Barton, and Elver. I think Mama will try to keep Elver with her because he's the baby, only two, but if you hurry you could probably get Hershal or Barton. Maybe you could get them both. They don't eat as much as most boys and have nice manners. Barton is very good with dogs if you have one and Hershal can fix things. They're both very nice boys. I like boys better than girls. Except Tillie. She's very nice. She can cook and likes to wash dishes. Me, I hate cooking and everything that's connected with it. I'd just as soon not eat if I have to wash the dishes. I am a very finicky eater. I only like fresh strawberries and goose livers."

"Me, I like things like truffles and caviar," said Mr. Sistrunk. "And crepes suzette. I am very good at making crepes suzette. We always have them at Thanksgiving and Christmas. Have you ever tasted this delicacy?"

"No," I answered, and for the benefit of the situation put some strength in my voice and jaw. "Tillie will eat anything," I said. "So will Barton and Hershal. They're all so little though; what they eat you could put in a gnat's eye. Me, I'm an expensive kid. I eat like a horse. I grow about five inches a month so I have to have new clothes every time you turn around and I have a lot of ailments. You see these spots on my legs?"

The Sistrunks leaned to look at my leg spots. "Freckles," said Mrs. Sistrunk. "I had them on my legs when I was a child. Don't worry about them. They'll fade as you grow older. Mine did."

This place was known merely as the Children's Home and was filled to overflowing with such a ragtag and bobtail assortment of little people as to make the mind boggle. Some had ugly ways and were tough. They fought in the stairways and hallways. They marked and cut the walls, hurled things through windows, and cut their bedsheets to shreds. At night they had nightmares and screamed. There were others with daisy faces who crept through the days doing only as they were told, without ever raising their eyes or speaking. The ladies in charge raced around in a dither; it was hard to get the attention of one of them even long enough to ask a simple question.

The Sistrunks and I sat in the bare, sunny room that had been assigned to us for our meeting and I, who had been afraid for about a month, felt the fear in me suddenly slip from its binding and fall sideways. Before that I had been able to hang on to it, hiding it from Tillie and Hershal and Barton by being bossy and acting breezy. When I saw them in the halls I would run up to them and say, "Hey, guys, what d'you know? Not anything? Well, nothing's changed then, has it? Hey, I got some news for you. I got permission to call up that old galoot judge who sentenced Daddy and guess what? He may not have to stay where he is the full time. If he's good he might get out earlier. Isn't that wonderful?"

They would stand in front of me with their socks bagging down over the tops of their shoes and the tears running out of their eyes. One of them would say, "We hate him. A father shouldn't steal and be put in jail."

I would say, "He didn't steal. He only received things that were stolen. The judge said that. Daddy didn't know those men were thieves. If you had a restaurant and you needed a cash register and a new stove and somebody came up to you and said they had one they'd sell you cheap, you'd take it, wouldn't you?"

"And then he talked back to the judge—"

"Because he was innocent. Don't you talk back to people when they say you've done something you haven't?"

"He hit those policemen—"

"Because they were mean and nasty. He didn't know they were policemen. They weren't wearing uniforms and didn't say what they were till after the fight. Look here, guys, you've got to remember things like they happened. Things could be a lot worse, that's what I'm thinking and that's what you should think. The world hasn't come to an end and nobody's dead."

"Don't call me a guy," said Tillie.

"If somebody was to chop your head off, you'd say you was better off without it," said Hershal.

"We don't want to talk to you," said Barton. "Leave us alone."

I took them by their arms and pushed them over against the wall and was hateful to them. "Pull up your socks and stop that sniveling. You say you don't want to talk to me? Well, maybe I don't want to talk to you either but I have to because we're related and I'm the oldest and the boss. I want you to do like I do. Just take every day—"

"The next time it's cold and you want me to warm up your side of the bed I'm not going to do it," said Tillie, making a desperate promise. "I just can't stand it anymore, the way you always find excuses for everything bad that happens to us. It's not normal."

I spoke the frozen truth to them. I said, "I *have* to find excuses for everything bad that happens to us. If I didn't I'd fall to pieces like you do."

"You aren't human," said Hershal. "You make us sick. Go away. Leave us alone."

I wasn't able to translate myself to them. They ran away from me and stayed away. All of them, because they were younger, were quartered in other buildings but I saw them sometimes on the playground. They stared at me and turned their backs. They were mad at the world. With the passing of each day I observed their faces growing thinner and their periwinkle eyes reassured me of their awful anxieties.

The sun was on the floor of the bare, little room where the Sistrunks and I were holding our little meeting. In the corridors and upstairs, over our heads, people were walking, running, jumping. It was the month of May, clear and warm and sound carried easily. From the high wires stretched along the utility poles across the road from the Children's Home there was a humming and on some faraway border of sound a car played a musical horn.

Looking at the Sistrunks, I thought, "They have to know my story, else they wouldn't be here. And since they are here, they can't be selfish. If only they could see Tillie and the boys and me together they would know we can't be separated, not even for a little while. I will tell them. I will just say, 'Now see here. We are a loving family and we are already too much separated without making it worse. You are hungry for me, I can see that. Well, I am hungry for my brothers and sister. I am not worried about Mama. She is going to keep house for a doctor and his wife and Elver will be with her. But the rest of us have got to stay together. You must see that. We will be good and we will make it fun for you. Our fun doesn't cost anything. I write plays and the rest of them act them out. Year before last we did *The First Flag*. Tillie was Martha Washington and Hershal was George. Mama taught us all how to dance the minuet. She played the piano for us. Tum, dum dum dum dum dum de dum. We had wigs made out of wood shavings; so pretty. And last year we did one about a creepy old guy who was actually a human fly. I made Barton a black costume with some long, scary antlers sticking up out of his head and when Tillie and I pulled him up off the floor with some invisible wires, everybody screamed.' "

"Delpha," said Mr. Sistrunk.

"Barton was so funny in the fly play," I said out loud. "I stuffed his antlers with wieners. We ate them afterward."

"Delpha," said Mrs. Sistrunk. "Your sister and brothers were placed in other foster homes early this morning. They've already gone."

"No," I said. "They wouldn't. Not without saying good-bye to me. They were mad at me because I had to act toward them like I wasn't so worried but they wouldn't go away without saying good-bye to me. I think you must be mistaken. If you will excuse me for a minute I will just go and ask one of the ladies in charge."

"Delpha, wait a minute, dear. You must . . . . Delpha, they are all going to be in good homes. They will write to you and maybe we can invite them to come and visit you. Maybe, on weekends, they might be allowed to stay over-night. We'll have some parties."

I untied my hair bow and let my hair fall down around my face for I didn't want what I felt to be seen. I was cold and had to hug myself and gasp once or twice because what I felt was crushing me.

The musical horn on the faraway border of sound was again tinkling its gay little tune and presently Mr. and Mrs. Sistrunk took me from the bare room and the Children's Home.

None of this was anybody's fault.

The Sistrunks lived in an odd house that once had been the property of a famous magician. It stood away from the town at the end of a winding road and had marvelous old mahogany walls and floors, cool to the touch, that were rich and gloomy. At its front there lay a delph blue pond and at night when the wind blew across this water its door and locks, half a century old, squeaked and rattled.

Mr. Sistrunk was not a thing-fixer and Mrs. Sistrunk was not a dirt or lint chaser. They had rooms of books and could sit for great stretches of time utterly absorbed in what they read while the dishwater grew cold and the leakings throughout the house caused bits of plaster to fall. In the early hours of my first, complete day with them there was a goose-drowner—a wild, dark rain—and the electricity failed. The Sistrunks set three candles in holders and lighted them and the wind, gusting down the kitchen chimney, blew soot across the hearth.

"We'll clean the house as soon as the storm is done," said Mrs. Sistrunk. "But while it's here let's just be lazy and talk. What is your favorite subject, Delpha?"

"Oh," I replied. "Old times, I guess. Whenever it rains I always think of them. And dream of them."

Mrs. Sistrunk poured three glasses of cold milk, put three cold, hard seed rolls on a plate and sat down. She pushed a glass dish toward me. "Have some of my tangerine butter with your roll. It's the only thing I know how to make decently. I hope your thoughts and dreams about old times don't make you sad."

"Oh, no," I said, wanting a quick correction of this. "Because I know there are better ones coming. I always put that in my mind when anything bad happens. I always say to myself, Delpha, old kid, it could be a lot worse. You could have been born with a stovepipe for a head and nothing to put in it and then you wouldn't feel *anything*. So then I go on about my business and pretty soon it's over, whatever it is that's bad and sad."

"Optimism is a wonderful strength," observed Mr. Sistrunk. "Would you like some more milk?"

"No, thanks. It's funny you should use that word; it's one of my daddy's favorites. He always says it enlarges life to be cheerful. Isn't that beautiful?"

"It's noble," said Mrs. Sistrunk simply. "Would you

17

like another roll? I'm sorry I can't offer you a nice boiled egg for your breakfast."

"I don't like eggs," I said. "I only eat them to be polite. Have you ever seen a chicken with coccidiosis? Well, you know, before my daddy got to be a restaurant owner he was a poultry farmer and he had two hundred chickens and they all got coccidiosis. We tried everything we could think of but they all died. Now none of us likes eggs. My daddy's not going to be a cook anymore when he gets out of jail. He's going to be a preacher."

"How interesting," said the Sistrunks. "What denomination?"

"I dunno. He might start up a new one. We've tried all the old ones; we've been everything. Baptists, Methodists, Episcopalians, Presbyterians, Catholics, Seventh-Day Adventists, and Jehovah's Witnesses. Do you know the trouble with these religions? Well, I'll tell you what their trouble is. They try to make you think that this life is just some kind of a dream and that when you wake up you'll be sorry that you've had a good time and enjoyed it. My dad doesn't think people should feel guilty when they enjoy things. He wants them to. He wants everybody to rejoice and celebrate every day they're here. He doesn't want to wait for the hereafter. He wants everybody to be as much as he can be, right now, and help his neighbors be as much as *they* can be, too."

"Your father must be a thinker," said Mr. Sistrunk.

"Oh, he is! A reader, too. He didn't have a chance to go to school very much but he's awfully educated from books he's read. He's a sweet man. He'll make a good minister. It's what he's always wanted to be and now he's got his chance. He isn't going to waste his time. He's going to study hard while he's locked up. He's going to learn to be a minister from one of those schools that teaches by mail and get a diploma and then when we're all together again we're going to have a good life."

The light from the three candles on the long, spavined table was flickering; there was another draft in the chimney. A sodden fig branch swept feebly against a pane and we listened to the wind whistling along the sharp roof-angles of the old house.

Mrs. Sistrunk spooned tangerine butter from the jar, punched a little hole in its glistening center and filled it with milk. She ate this and grinned at me, flashing her soft dimples. "I have some strange eating habits," she said. "I hope they won't bother you."

"No," I answered. "I used to know a sweet old lady who liked banana sandwiches. I used to go down to her house every Sunday afternoon for tea. She was from England."

"You were good friends?"

"Oh, yes. Very good friends."

"You have a lot of friends, haven't you?"

"Oh, yes. Everybody."

"What's your favorite school subject?"

"My favorite subject? I dunno. Math is easiest for me. It's so quick and easy for me my teachers don't believe it. It's like I was born with the answers already in my head. Sometimes I have a feeling I've lived before. In some other place. In some other time."

There was a sudden, exceptionally sharp whoosh of wind in the chimney and the yellow candle flames were stretched thin for just a second. The storm lasted well into the middle of that afternoon and during this important time it was revealed to me that I had lived my entire life in ignorance of my true self.

The Sistrunks were both practitioners of the ancient art of astrology. Every morning they read their horoscopes in the newspaper and every month they bought horoscope magazines at the drugstore. They said it was a pastime that occupied the attentions of millions of people in the civilized world and whether it was only for fun or a thing to really be believed in was a matter of personal choice. The stars, they said, influenced humans and human affairs and each person is born under his own particular star sign and is ruled by his own planet and inherits his own particular star name.

"What is your date of birth?" they asked.

"January twenty-fifth," I replied.

"Do you happen to know the hour?"

How could I know the hour? Probably not even Honey Bunch, which is the nickname for Mama, even knows that. When it is possible, she likes to forget the time and lie abed in the mornings, reading stories to Elver. For both of them noon can come and it can go. When they are alone, they eat animal crackers and oranges for their lunch and in the afternoons plant seeds and play learning games. Honey Bunch is not lazy but she is not fond of tracking the hours.

The Sistrunks were looking at me and because I was a guest in their home and owed them something for their hospitality I supplied them with my version of the details of my birth:

"It seems like it might have been about two o'clock in the morning. It seems like I can remember part of it. It was raining like it is now and black as pitch. There was a big gold bird sitting on the windowsill, an eagle or something like that. And my dad was all dressed up. He could hardly wait for me, and all the neighbors were there eating little cakes and sandwiches. They were having a party. Well, sir, the first thing I heard was that bird. When I was born he shrieked. You know the way eagles shriek? And somebody threw him a sandwich and he flew off into the trees. Nobody ever saw him again. They named me Delpha Louise and everybody sang songs and then they went home and that's all."

The Sistrunks were fascinated with this account. They skipped from the kitchen and skipped back, lugging a stack of books. They slipped through the pages of these and pounced on a delightful truth. "Aha! We knew it. You are a native of the fixed star Aquarius. The planet Uranus rules you. Oh, Delpha, you are so lucky. You have so many brilliant possibilities."

"I have?"

"Marvelous ones. You could be anything you chose to be. Have you thought about a profession yet?"

"Yes. I've decided what I'm going to be about a hundred times already."

"Do you like poetry?"

"Love it. I write it sometimes."

"Stories?"

"All kinds. I wish I could eat words, I like them so much."

"Do you like the dance?"

"Mmmmmmmmmmm!"

"The ocean?"

"So big. I wonder what's under it. I'd like to be one of those people that study oceans."

"Are you a nature lover?"

"Mmmmmmmmm. Clouds. Birds. Trees. I hug trees."

"Delpha, do you know your star name?"

"No," I replied. "Nobody ever told it to me."

"You're a Water Bearer," said the Sistrunks most gravely and then their smiles exploded and the wind at the door blew it open and all but my candle flame was extinguished.

CAPRICORN
THE GOAT
DECEMBER 22ND THROUGH
JANUARY 20TH

Saturnian loser who wins
More firsts than lasts.

TWO

I should tell some things about the town of Chinquapin Cove and the people who lived in it. This little place was held away from the rest of the world by a ring of soft hills. On the sides of these there were thick clusters of trees where gray crows lived and early each morning these birds left their roosting places and came to fly over the town. They watched the people hurrying from their homes to the shoe factory which employed a large number of them. The narrow, cobbled streets, many close to a hundred years old, would be wet and slippery when there was dew or rain or frost and this was a small danger but the people could not think of complaining for the factory owner also was the controller of the town.

The citizens of Chinquapin Cove seemed a dreary lot. They were never threatened with a shortage of work because the shoes they made were in constant demand and were shipped to all parts of the country but the rooms in which they toiled were cheerless and ill-ventilated and there were other undesirable conditions. There was dust and the stream which ran past the back of the factory was polluted with all kinds of waste matter. The factory had a tin roof and its thin walls were not insulated so the inside temperatures were never comfortable. The employees ate their lunches at their benches and watched the clock. They worked only for money and were afraid to go to their employer and say, "Look here, this is wrong and that is wrong and we want it changed; if you don't change things we will quit." For there was no other work in the town for them and their imaginations could not allow them to consider strange places and untried things.

As all people, these people had the gift of dreams and they could think of better things for themselves and their families but no one had ever actually said to them that they could be more than they were. So on each weekday morning they plodded to the shoe factory and on each weekday night plodded home again. On Sundays they attended to the awful importance of preparing for the hereafter. They went to church and listened attentively to their ministers and afterward each, though uninspired, said, "I feel better. That was a good sermon. Isn't the weather nice?" Their relations with each other were so vague and dull all they could find to talk about was the weather. In Chinquapin Cove weather was the most talked about subject.

I left the protection of the Sistrunks and their home on a June day that was filled with strong sun. By 10 A.M. it had drawn all the night moisture from the grass that grew in the Sistrunks' yard and the scent from the sweet bubbybushes, flowering along the front fence, was one that I would forever remember. Away on the surrounding horizon the gray crows glided in circles above the hills and the Sistrunks stood in their doorway waving good-bye. I would never see them again for they were packing to move to Michigan where, hopefully, better opportunities would present themselves.

My father came after me in a little white car that was actually more like a small bus. It was rusty around the doors and windows and there was a hole in its dashboard panel where once a radio had been. Even so it seemed to run as well as other cars I had known. Its imperfections were hardly worth mentioning.

After a year and thirty days my family and I were going to again be allowed to live together. We had a house in which to live, everybody was healthy, we were on the threshold of a new and improved life. My father was now Reverend Green and had a beautiful gold and white parchment diploma to prove it. He was handsomer than before. A little too thin but with a look of peace and radiance about him. Driving himself and me away from the Sistrunks in the little car-bus he said, "Well, Delpha, this is a morning to remember, isn't it?"

"Yes, sir," I said. "I always will."

"You're the last one to be rounded up. The others are all waiting for us."

"I know. Mama phoned me three hours ago. So did Tillie and Hershal and Barton."

"The Sistrunks are nice people, aren't they?"

"They're lovely and they were good to me. They let Tillie and Hershal and Barton come to visit me as often as they could. Mama and Elver too. I wish they weren't moving away but they can't stand it here any longer. To them this town is like a place in the dark ages. Mrs. Sistrunk says it's weird."

"Honey Bunch bought this spiffy car for us," said my father. "Do you like it?"

"It's cute," I said. "I like it better than any car I've ever ridden in. Daddy, are you really a real minister now? Are you really going to start up a church of your own?"

"Yes."

"I think that's wonderful. All those good ideas you're going to tell people about. What's absurdity of possessions? I wrote and asked you but you never answered my question."

"I am sorry," said my father. "I will explain it to you now."

"You said people were too concerned with possessions."

"They are. They certainly are, considering that they come to this world with nothing and must go from it with nothing. In between it's good to have things that make our lives better but there are some people who let their greed for outward possessions run away with them. They spend so much of their lives collecting things and then guarding them that they don't have time for anything else. It's silly. A better word is absurd."

"Mr. Sistrunk's uncle died and left him two thousand dollars and he gave it all to the Children's Home," said I and hugged the stack of books in my lap. They were presents from the Sistrunks and were concerned with the study of how to recognize the individual human being according to his date of birth and this was the most startling, illuminating thing I had ever encountered. Now it lay within my power to understand and influence, hopefully for the best, every person I met. I had to tell my father about this:

"Daddy, you see these books? They're just about the best things I ever read. They tell about how everybody's got a sun sign and how his nature is influenced by the movement of the sun, moon, and planets. Did you know we all had zodiac names? Tillie is Cancer, the Crab and I'm Aquarius, the Water Bearer and a girl I know—I call her Purple Bubble Gum—is Capricorn, the Goat. Capricorn people are born between December twenty-second and January the twentieth. They just hate anything that isn't honest but Purple Bubble Gum didn't know that until I told her so. She used to steal money from her mother and sometimes she'd get caught and there'd be an awful fuss. She doesn't do it anymore. Do you know the trouble with most people? They don't understand themselves. Their minds are just ignorant about themselves so they run around doing the wrong things all their lives and then when it comes time for their turn to die they say, 'What happened? I made too many mistakes. I want to go back and do it over again.' Only they can't because by that time it's too late."

My father said, "I can hardly wait to meet Purple Bubble Gum." By this time we were going through the main, business part of the town and he was having to watch more carefully.

Said I, "Her eyes make you think of our nation's flag. True blue. She never lets anybody know her feelings. Capricorns never do. They worry a lot but they never let anybody know."

"I will tell you something I have learned about worry," said my father. "It is the least worthwhile of all occupations because the things we worry about the most almost never happen. Worry is only good for two things I can think of. It grows gray hair before you're ready for it and keeps doctors busy. When anybody tells me they're worried about this little thing or that little thing I am always reminded of a story I read once. About a man traveling across the Sahara Desert carrying a raincoat."

"He must have been a fool," I said. "Sometimes years go by and it doesn't rain in the Sahara Desert."

"He was a worrier," said my father.

Our place of new residence looked as if its builder had started out with one plan and changed his mind several times. It had a high, peaked front and a long, low back. There was a confusion of big, square rooms and little lopped ones with doors which did not connect and windows which had to be propped because the weights in their old-fashioned sashes were broken. There was vine and bush leafage at every pane and this made the rooms dark. Their painted floors were scarred and their walls gave off an odor of mildew. In the corners of the yard there were piles of storm-wrack—broken branches and long, blown tangles of Spanish moss.

This place stood, awkward and alone, in the center of an otherwise uninhabited block and to me its ugly, perishing sight was at first a little heart-sinking for we had always lived in brighter, better places. But then, because I was the oldest child and had to set the example for the younger ones, I said, "Oh, it'll be nice when we get it cleaned and fixed." There was some good excitement in the first few minutes of our reunion. Everybody kissed and hugged each other.

This new home of ours was also going to be the meetinghouse for the members of The Church of Blessed Hope, no denomination. The two big front rooms would be fine for that, said Honey Bunch. And said wouldn't it be interesting to live in a house that was half church.

"Interesting," said Tillie and Hershal and Barton, and looked at their feet and each other, hiding what they truly felt. Again, because I was the oldest, it was up to me to ease the strain of the moment. I said to Mama that it would be interesting *and* wonderful to live in a house that was half church. This comment accomplished its aim. Honey Bunch sang as she made a stack of sandwiches while Daddy went after three kinds of fancy ice cream. We had a small celebration and after this there was all the cleaning and straightening to be done. Elver was the only one allowed to goof off. He spent the entire afternoon shouting words of encouragement to the workers: "Faster! Go faster! Work for the night is coming!" He popped in and out so fast and so often that finally he had to be ordered to the kitchen and given the job of arranging the pots and pans in the cabinet beneath the sink. He hung a kettle over his head and blissfully sang and his voice was spooky—it sounded a thousand miles away and Honey Bunch laughed and said Elver had a fine choir voice and that when the time came it would be enlisted.

On her head Tillie wore a little straw hat with a cluster of glossy plastic berries attached to its crown. It looked like a relic from somebody's attic but Tillie would only say that it was a present from a friend and refused to take it off. All during the day's activities she didn't remove it from her head for one second. Hershal and Barton made fun of it, saying she looked more like a monkey than a monkey in it and she threw a bucket of soapy water and a broom at them.

At dusk everybody was dog-tired from all the yard cleaning and pruning and all the furniture moving and scrubbing. We were so tired we had to force ourselves to our supper of creamed chipped beef on biscuits and afterward Tillie, Hershal, Barton, and I went outside and sat in the cooling grass. The light was failing and my brothers, sister, and I sat without speaking and watched a flock of birds go across the waning sky in a wing-to-wing train.

Finally Tillie removed her hat, placing it on the hump of one updrawn knee. She sat facing the front of the ugly house and after a while expressed a solemn opinion. "It's the craziest thing of all," she said. "First the chickens and then the restaurant and now this. Does anybody besides me remember the chickens?"

"Sholey," said Barton. "I for one most sholey do. Squawk, squaaaaaawk, squawk, all the time squaaaaaawk. How we had to doctor them when they got sick—"

"And then they all died," said Hershal.

"And then we were broke again," said Barton. "In that terrible place. Remember how cold it used to get there?"

"Then we had the restaurant," said Tillie. "I hated it. I am never going to eat another hamburger or look at another bowl of chili. But at least we were respectable then for a while." Her fingers stroked the cherries on her hat and her voice lingered on her words, vague and innocent.

Said I, "Wait a minute. Now wait just a minute. We're respectable now. What makes you think we're not?"

Tillie did not promptly supply the answer to this question. She lifted her hat from her knee and set it on her head. It slipped down over one eye and she straightened it, the cherries in its crown darkly wobbling. She bent her head to her knees and plucked a blade of grass. After a couple of minutes she said, "The Church of Blessed Hope makes me think it. I wish somebody could assure me where that name comes from. What will this church of our father's teach? Does anybody here know that?"

"It is going to teach the way for understanding between all people," I said. "You heard Daddy explain it, same as the rest of us."

"I don't," said Tillie, "understand that. I don't understand what trouble he's after and how he means to fix it."

I was on uncertain ground myself for it is one thing sometimes to hear words and very much another to understand their meanings. All I could say to Tillie was, "It's a new religion. Don't worry about it. Look at the stars. Aren't they beautiful? So far away but so bright."

Tillie looked up at the appearing stars. "I don't feel good. Seems to me like I feel another of my attacks of rheumatism coming on. I hope I don't have to work as hard tomorrow as I did today. My bones feel like they've got the fever. It'd be so nice if I could just stay in bed all day tomorrow. All last year when I lived with Mr. and Mrs. Mast she used to let me stay in bed when I didn't feel good. She's such a lovely person. Her husband does law work for Mr. Merlin Choate. Have you ever seen Mr. Merlin Choate up close, Delpha?"

"Close enough," I replied. I had not then and never had had any real interest in the owner of the Choate Shoe Factory. His smile was so pale and meaningless. Every day he ate his lunch on the veranda of the Choate Hotel and the people passing beneath him in the street always looked up to eagerly acknowledge him. It was embarrassing to watch.

"Mr. Mast is Mr. Merlin Choate's lawyer," said Tillie, starting one of her long, wandering monologues. "Mr. Choate wants to get a divorce from Mrs. Choate now and one night when I was staying with the Masts, Mr. Choate came to our house. He's been married to Mrs. Choate for forty-three years and says he's tired of it now. He's doing everything he can' to get young again but Mrs. Choate doesn't want him young. She wants him old."

"Mrs. Choate owns this place we're living in," observed Hershal. "I went with Mama to rent it from her. I think she's loony."

In the gray-black darkness, Tillie's face whitely gleamed. "She's sure got strong lungs. That night Mr. Choate came to talk to Mr. Mast about getting a divorce from her she stood out in front of our house and beat on the fence with a stick and screamed at Mr. Choate till he got sick. Here's how she sounded: 'Merlin! Merlin! You come outa there now. You and I have got some things to settle and I want to get it done. Merlin, if you in there gettin' a new will drawed or if you in there figurin' out a way to get me sent to the crazy house you better think twice 'fore you sign anything. People's eyes ain't painted on. People know I'm just an old, helpless woman. You old too, Merlin. Now I know that's a painful thing to hear but you got to face up to it, Merlin. Come go home with me now, Merlin. It's late and I shouldn't be out in this night air. Neither should you. Merlin! Merlin! You hear me, Merlin?' "

"That is a sad story," I said. "Two people who have been married forty-three years should just love each other and be nice. Maybe they should never have gotten married in the first place. Maybe they have the wrong zodiac signs for each other."

"Oh, zodiac signs," said Tillie and, holding her hat aloft, twirling it, lay in the grass.

Said I, "In the olden days, kings and queens had astrologers to tell them what to do. It was a royal art. There might be more to it than you think, Tillie. More than I think also. It's very complicated. And interesting."

"If you believe in it then I don't know you," said Tillie. "It's superstitious, that's what it is. And I sure hope you haven't got in mind to run around all over town asking people what date they were born. We're strange enough living here in this crazy church-house to which I'm sure nobody in his right mind is ever going to come except just once to look. I am thinking about changing my name to Smith or Jones. Which do you think sounds best? Tallullah Jones or Tallullah Smith?"

"You'll be sorry if you disown the name of Green," I warned. "You're going to be sorry you made fun of our little church-house too. Pretty soon we're going to have a congregation bigger than all others in Chinquapin Cove put together."

"I wish I had a lot of money," said Tillie. "I wish I could think of something to invent. Mr. Mast invents things in his spare time. Someday he's going to strike it rich with one of his inventions and then he's going to tell Mr. Merlin Choate to take his old shoe factory and go jump in one of the oceans. And take Mrs. Choate with him."

"If you want to invent something you will," I said. "People born under your sign make good inventors because they have lots of imagination."

"Mrs. Choate scares me just to look at her," said Tillie. "She's got a map on her that'd curdle the devil's blood. It's no wonder to me Mr. Choate wants a divorce from her. She ought to go buy herself a new face or at least get her old one fixed up a little. That's what I'd do if I had all her money."

Not wanting to get into a conversation about money, which is a useless subject when you don't have any, I made no answer. I looked at the sky. Chinquapin Cove and all that surrounded it lay sloth in the deepening night. The stars on the farthest rim of the horizon blinked and winked.

GEMINI

THE TWINS

MAY 22ND THROUGH JUNE 21ST

A quicksilver kaleidoscope
Paired with mercurial Mercury.

THREE

We opened our church doors to the public on the last Sunday in that June and, according to my knowledge of them, not any who attended the inauguration could be labeled normal. All had something a little amiss in their lives.

During my stay with the Sistrunks I had compiled a little secret study of many of the citizens of Chinquapin Cove, listing their names in a notebook in alphabetical order (so as not to show any preference) and jotting interesting facts concerning them beside their names. It had been a harmless pastime with really no purpose except as an aid to sharpen my powers of people-perception which might, someday, enable me to be a better teacher. Or a more eloquent poetess. Or a more superior astrologer.

During a quiet period in this Sunday afternoon I slipped away to study my secret record of the people in Chinquapin Cove for now it appeared that it might, after all, be of some real, immediate use but I was not to have any privacy in doing this. Tillie came to snoop and spy and couldn't very well be ordered from the room because half of it was rightfully hers.

Because it was Sunday Tillie had, that morning, given careful attention to her hair but only to the sides and front. A long, brown bang of it lay smoothly across her forehead and two fat buns of it, run through with crinkly hairpins, covered her ears. The back of it was all snarled and fuzzed. A pearly pink button sewn with red thread had been added to the brim of her hat. She had a sometimes odd contempt for the comforts of convenience and sat astraddle the foot railing of her bed eating Saltine crackers. "Sundays kill me," she said. "Whoever invented them should be tarred and feathered. Are you doing something special or are you just sitting in here mooning?"

"I'm just sitting in here mooning," I replied. "And I don't want to be talked to especially."

"Whatcha reading?"

"Poetry."

"Read me some. I might like it today."

I lifted my notebook so as to hide my face from Tillie's vision and read:

"Hearts entwined
And arms too

The young lovers awaited their destiny.
'Twas an old lady
Smothered in lace
Who spake it, saying
Nevermore."

Tillie laughed. "Oh, my conscience."

"And He and She smiled sadly
While seeming to agree.
They had a secret and 'twas this:
Their Prince had come
And would set them free."

Tillie chewed a cracker and rubbed the button on her hat. "I don't understand poetry; I don't see how anybody can. Hershal and Barton have gone to hunt for pop bottles. I was just out with them but it was so hot I came back. When we get enough we're going to take them to a store and with the money we get for them we're going to buy a little battery and some wire and other stuff and invent a new kind of collection plate. It'll reward people when they're generous and scare them when they're not. Axe Aleywine only put in a quarter this morning and Betty Jean Swain only put in a dime. Isn't that chintzy?"

"I wish you wouldn't talk when you've got food in your mouth," I said. "Why don't you go someplace else to eat your crackers? I told you I didn't want to talk especially."

Indifferent to my disapproval of her eating habits, Tillie took a can of sardines from the hip pocket of her jeans, opened it with its little metal key, slid one of the slender, oily fish out on a cracker and popped it into her mouth. "This place gives me the creeps. I don't think so much of the church business. I think we're going to starve. We can't live on five dollars and forty cents a week; that's how much we took in this morning."

"I wish you'd hush. I'm trying to think."

"I think this church is going to flop," said Tillie, helping herself to another sardine-on-cracker. "Like our chicken business flopped and our restaurant. Some people go to church just for the singing but we can't even do that right. Ours was awful this morning without a piano. We need an organ or piano like the Baptist church has."

"We'll have one soon," I said, expressing a confidence that wouldn't stand too much scrutiny.

Tillie, who sometimes went on health binges, finished eating her crackers and sardines and, after a moment of consideration, drank the sardine oil. "Oil is good for people," she commented with only a faint grimace. "What were we speaking of? Oh, yes. As I was saying, I think our church is going to flop."

"Do you? I don't."

"I was watching the people who came this morning and I am sure not one person understood Daddy's speech."

"Sermon, Tillie. Not speech."

"Axe Aleywine and Betty Jean Swain didn't even listen. I think they just came so they could look at each other. They didn't arrive together; I was watching. Mrs. Mast told me Axe's mother won't let him marry Betty Jean. She won't even let Axe take Betty Jean to the movies. What was I speaking of? Oh, yes. As I was saying, I don't think anybody understood Daddy's speech this morning. I didn't. When he said everybody should experience the world and then they would experience God. And said if we would all be creative we'd stop being anxious about things. And that we could all be our own angels. I certainly would never know how to be my own angel and what's creative? I'm not creative. I don't know how to be and I'm sure nobody else who was in church this morning does either. They all work in the shoe factory."

"They know how to be creative," I said. "Anybody can be creative. All they have to do is understand themselves first."

"Oh, my conscience," said Tillie.

"It is true," I said, going to the dresser to search first through a box and then a drawer for any little spangle because I was going out on the town to make a few calls and wanted to look my best. I found a piece of black velvet which looked nice tied around my neck and a bright Japanese fan which, when unfurled, presented a charming picture of pretty little Japanese ladies in kimonos. The fan had been a gift from Mrs. Sistrunk and was one of my favorite possessions. I brushed my hair until it crackled and stood out from my head. Being nice, Tillie said it looked like spun sugar. I said, "When you understand yourself you are able to understand everybody else because when you are informed about yourself your heart enlarges. Then you see things you never saw before and can be creative."

"Oh, my conscience," said Tillie and rolled her eyes.

"Yes. You could find out what I am saying is the truest thing you ever heard if you wanted to, but of course if you just want to be like you are all your life that is your business. I am going out for a while. When Mama and Daddy wake up from their naps will you tell them please? I will be back in an hour or so."

"Sometimes," said Tillie, "I get the spookiest feeling you and I aren't related. You're creepy. It isn't just me has this feeling about you either. Everybody in our family has it. Mama says you scare her sometimes."

"She is joking," I said. "I could not possibly scare anybody even if I tried because that is one thing I do not know how to do." I gathered my fan and notebook and skipped from the room and house and out into the street. There was only a hobbled notion of what I was about in my mind. My ideas and reasons for their slippery forms had been hopping around in my brain for days now, coming and going so fast that all I could do was grab hold of their tail ends. Sometimes a realization of what I could do with them seemed so clear and possible but at other times appeared fuddled, beyond my reach and too complicated. One thing for certain stood out in my mind: Good things, more often than not, went without notice because they were not advertised and our church had not been advertised. My father, so quiet and tasteful, was not willing to shout what he believed from the rooftops. He preferred to believe that people would be drawn to his church by its simplicity and freshness and that they would tell their friends and so on and on until he had a full congregation.

This could not, I reflected, happen unless somebody made it happen. To be practical and help matters along a little, that was the thing to do. The order of the day.

I stepped off down the street, going to the far corner of it and turning into a neighborhood. I went past the houses steeped in Sabbath quiet.

At random I chose the home of Miss Pearl Drawhorne who lived in retirement with a sixty-year-old parrot named Fletcher. It was easy to imagine this spinster lady having been a secretary to Mr. Merlin Choate at the shoe factory for some forty-odd years, the way she had of spying on callers from behind her lace curtains, suspiciously sizing them up as if they were traveling salesmen with cheap, undesirable wares come to rob the boss of important time. She and her bird looked quite a bit alike, both with hawkish eyes and large, gaudy heads. Fletcher's head was brilliantly green and Miss Drawhorne's was glossy black, much too glossy black, and she had red apple cheeks. She was snippy and primpish and known to the people of the town and Fletcher as Miss Pearl. When I rapped on her door, Fletcher's voice responded first, shrieking, "Miss Pearl! Answer the door, fool! By jingo! Bless Pat! Oh, you're a caution! Bet your boots! Miss Pearl!"

And in a moment Miss Pearl opened the door and said, "Oh. Well, hello."

"On behalf of the pastor of The Church of Blessed Hope I am out making a few calls," I said. "Mercy, isn't it hot though? But your place looks so cool. That's why I turned in. I am Delpha Green, the daughter of Reverend Green."

"Really?" said Miss Pearl and she was not at all impressed. "I don't believe I . . . What church did you say?"

To give my hands something to do I held my unfurled

fan against my cheek. "The Church of Blessed Hope. Probably you haven't heard of it yet because it's new. If I am not interrupting something, may I come in and tell you about it?"

"Oh, I don't believe I'm interested," said Miss Pearl. "I'm a Baptist. Not a good one, I fear. Because of circumstances in my home I don't get out much. I must say I think it's rather unusual for a child . . . Does your father know you're out like this, dear? Did he send you?"

"No," I told her. "It's utterly my own idea. Probably it's childish. I don't know yet. But I just thought a church like ours needed to be advertised. You see, we believe in so many good things. When you experience the world then you experience God. That's one."

"True," said Miss Pearl with a hand on her bodice. "Come to think of it."

"And we believe in play. So many people think to just work all the time. My father says this was all right back in the olden days but now our land is so rich and everybody's bettered themselves so much they should learn to play more."

"My dear," said Miss Pearl. "These *are* the olden days in Chinquapin Cove. We're at least thirty years behind other towns this size. We're dead, that's what. All we're waiting for is for somebody to come cover us up."

"The flowers in your yard are so pretty," I said. It was an uncomfortable minute.

"The people in this town don't know how to play," observed Miss Pearl. "They only know how to work in the shoe factory. Mr. Merlin Choate better not catch anybody

42

playing. For all I know there's a city ordinance against it. There is if Merlin's thought of it."

I had to try to not let this visit be a waste. I said, "My father says everybody should celebrate every day as if it was going to be their last. He says they should be creative and then they'd forget their anxieties. I told my sister Tallullah —we call her Tillie—anybody can be creative if they understand themselves first. Because when you understand yourself then your heart enlarges and you understand everything."

"You have the strangest vocabulary," said Miss Pearl, staring. "Your eyes are so strange. Is one of them false?"

"No, ma'am. I was just born with one green and one blue, that's all. People have been asking me that since I was three years old. Do you know I can remember back to the time I was three years old? My father wasn't a minister then. He had a job but he hated it because his boss wouldn't even let the people who worked for him talk to each other. He just wanted them to keep their noses in their work and not look up until the bell rang for them to quit. On the day I was three years old my father came home at noon and said he wasn't going back to that job and Honey Bunch—that's my mother—made some cherry tarts and we had a party."

"I think you had better come in," said Miss Pearl and held the door open so that I could step inside. "Watch out for Fletcher; he's always underfoot. Your hair is really the most extraordinary color. Your mother doesn't bleach it, does she? No, don't use that chair. It's an antique. Sit on the sofa."

"Fool!" screamed Fletcher, dancing around.

43

"Wheeeeee!" He flew to Miss Pearl and tried to sit in her lap but she gently thumped his head with a finger and he said, "Ouch, fool!" and hopped down and waddled away.

"He's beautiful," I said, hoping for a pleasant little visit.

Miss Pearl was brushing her skirt and glaring after her bird. "That's right," she said to him. "Sit in the corner and keep your mouth shut. You open it one more time today and you'll wish you were dead."

"Oh, you're a caution!" said Fletcher, hunched in his corner.

To be polite I asked, "Where did you get him?"

Miss Pearl appeared to have only been waiting for somebody to come along and ask her that question on this day, the way she tore into the answer. "Where did I get him, what a question. I thought everybody in Chinquapin Cove knew. That fool Merlin Choate gave him to me the first Christmas I worked for him. That's been, oh goodness, forty-five years ago. I've been retired for five years. But to get back to Fletcher. Merlin and I had been having some differences. As a matter of fact I had tendered my resignation because he had hired me to be his secretary but then he expected me to be his bookkeeper too. I was doing the work of two people but only getting paid one salary and it was so little I wasn't even able to afford a decent coat or go to the movies. Not that I cared anything about movies—they were so cheap and vulgar even back in those days. It was just the principle of the thing. Merlin used to sit in his office with his teeth out and he'd dictate letters to me only I couldn't understand half of what he said so I'd get things wrong sometimes. And his wife, oh, my word, I won't even discuss her. Such a coarse woman. Merlin has been trying to divorce her for years but even as powerful as he is he can't wangle it. Don't ask me why. I guess in earlier times, before Merlin got to be such a hog about money, they were happy together. I don't know. It's a mess. This whole town is a mess and most of it can be laid at Merlin's door."

"Wheeeeee!" said Fletcher, hopping up and down in his corner. He didn't turn around.

Ignoring the bird and continuing her peculiar, disordered tale, Miss Pearl took up a bit of embroidery and began to stitch furiously. "I sound like I'm crazy and maybe I am. You would be crazy too if you had been cooped up here in this house with nobody but a bird to keep you company for forty-five years. I'm afraid to even go to the market for food because he screams when I do and when I get back something's always been destroyed. He's always mad at me about something. He tears up my magazines and newspaper, even my clothes. When I was working it was awful. I never knew what I'd find when I got home. People ask me why I don't get rid of him or at least lock him in a cage. I couldn't; that would be inhuman. Of course, he isn't human. I don't understand why I can't do it. Other people could and it wouldn't bother them one bit. I don't understand myself sometimes."

Seated on Miss Pearl's satin sofa I furled and unfurled my fan. I watched Fletcher who still stood with his face to the wall. He was a little tattered as old birds must be, yet there was still something youthful about him, the way he lifted first one foot and then the other, examining his scaly toes, seeming to be fascinated with the way he could make them wiggle. Miss Pearl's hair was so stiff and sooty black; probably it was dyed. There was something about her that age had not yet consumed. The skin of her face was as smooth as my own and she didn't allow her back to slump.

"You were going to tell me about your church," said Miss Pearl, snipping threads with a little pair of scissors. "But now that I've asked you in, I don't think I want to hear about it. Churches depress me a little. I believe in God and the hereafter but sometimes it seems to me I just don't want to hear another word about what is going to happen to me in the hereafter. Sometimes it seems to me like my life is something of a waste. For some reason I've never really experienced the world. I've always just done exactly what other people wanted me to do. That fool bird there, for instance. Forty-five years I've had of him."

"Fool!" muttered Fletcher.

"He's beautiful," I said. "He looks a little bit like you; probably because you've been companions for so long. Miss Pearl, just now I had the funniest feeling about you. It was as if I was looking at two people; the old person you are now and the young one you used to be. That's the true sign of a Gemini person. Miss Pearl, would you mind to tell me if you were born between the dates of May twenty-second and June twenty-first?"

"Why, yes," said Miss Pearl, looking up. "My birthday is the eighth of June."

"Aha!" I said. "I knew it! Isn't it funny how I could tell? But not so funny either because I've been studying astrology for over a year now. And people. Miss Pearl, you

46

are a Twin. Twins is the sign for Gemini people. Mercury is your ruling planet. Have you seen mercury in a thermometer? That silver stuff? It's so beautiful and quick. Miss Pearl, according to your sign you are a very creative person. Probably you make presents for people on their birthdays and write pretty poems to go with them. And you're so kind; that's why you can't lock Fletcher in a cage. And the reason you worked for Mr. Merlin Choate so long—"

"I hate him," said Miss Pearl, interrupting. "He's a wicked man. Never go near him. Cover your face when you pass him in the street. Never invite him to your church. Of course, he'd never go anyway; he only donates to churches. He thinks people love him for his donations but they don't. They hate him. Everybody."

"I wonder what sign he is," I said, and Miss Pearl yanked her piece of embroidery from its hoop and answered. "His birthday is November the eighteenth for whatever that's worth. I don't believe in astrology. Of course I have never given it much thought or read anything on the subject. It's mostly hocus-pocus, I think."

"You might be right," I said.

"It isn't polite of you to droop your eyes like that when you're talking with people," said Miss Pearl in a little sharp, rebuking tone. "I like to see people's eyes when I'm talking with them."

I said, "Oh, excuse me," and then tactfully changed the subject. Telling Miss Pearl then of my year with the Sistrunks, weaving an entertaining story about it. And Miss Pearl gave it much attention, saying, "Yes, yes. Go on. Oh, they sound positively brilliant. I would not have thought to

47

carry my shoes to any social gathering. I always have to be dull and wear mine."

"They wanted their feet to look nice when they got there," I said, indulging myself in a conversational orgy. "They didn't like social doings much though. They had a big telescope and we used to sit out on the lawn in the evenings and look at the moon and stars. Mrs. Sistrunk said they made her think of religion and science, all at once and all together. We used to study plants. Mr. Sistrunk said it made sense to him to think if nature grew spring plants, then summer ones, then autumn ones, and then winter ones, humans must be the same way. How we are must be according to what month we were born."

"You say the Sistrunks write to you?" inquired Miss Pearl.

"Oh, sure. We could never give each other up."

"If the next letter you get from them isn't confidential I'd like to see it," said Miss Pearl. "All the people I know now and have ever known are duller than pith and yesterday's news."

Toward the end of this visit, which lasted much longer than I had intended, Fletcher was suddenly seized with a violent fit of coughing and Miss Pearl ran to pick him up and had to give him three teaspoons of rum, which to him was cough syrup. While she was doctoring him she promised him all sorts of things: all the bananas he could eat, a fresh supply of peanuts and sunflower seeds, a little walk as soon as the heat of the day was over.

"If you should walk past our church," I said, taking my

leave, "both of you would be welcome to come in even if it was only for a minute."

Miss Pearl couldn't make any reply to this invitation because Fletcher had recovered, darting suddenly to Miss Pearl's embroidery. He seized it in his bill and ran from the room with it and Miss Pearl chased after him and there were his high screams and cackling laughter: "Oh, Miss Pearl! You're a caution! Ouch! Bless Pat! Ouch, fool!"

SAGITTARIUS

THE ARCHER

NOVEMBER 23RD THROUGH
DECEMBER 21ST

Verbal arrow of malice not meant.
Nor was it enthusiastic Jupiter's intent.

FOUR

For some uncounted number of weeks my family and I lived without outside interferences, going about our own purposes steadily and in the highest of faith and though our star of prosperity did not fall into our laps exactly or dazzle much brighter at least it did not altogether disappear.

There was a family of ten named Leaptrot needing the services of a minister one weekday afternoon. Their oldest daughter with the lovely name of Autumn Lea wanted to quietly marry her childhood sweetheart. So, with all of the Leaptrots and all the members of the sweetheart's family and all of us Greens assembled in The Church of Blessed

51

Hope, the wedding words were said by my father and the gold ring, trembling in the groom's hand, was dropped and lost for a moment. Elver found it. The groom was so scared-looking and had the queer name of Neppie Nation and his father had to keep telling him what to do: "You can kiss the bride now, Neppie. She's all yours. That little 'un there on the floor is your sister-in-law now, Neppie; watch you don't step on her. Pay the preacher, Neppie."

"Oh, yes," said Neppie, gazing frozen-faced at his father. He slid his hand in his breast pocket, withdrew a white envelope and tried to give it to his father.

"Boy," said Neppie's father, "you got to get hold of yourself. I'm not the preacher; I'm your father. Pay the preacher and let's go."

"You are the prettiest bride I ever saw," I said to Autumn Lea. "Thank you for letting me hold your bouquet. Through every various turn of your married life I hope they will all be tender and joyful. Come worship with us next Sabbath if you've nothing better to do."

Autumn Lea accepted her bridal bouquet from my hands and said, "You should wear sunglasses. Your eyes make me nervous and so does the way you talk."

"I know," I said, sympathizing with her. "But when you get to know me better you won't notice either one. Your mother explained to me where you and Neppie are going to live. How soon will you be through with your honeymoon?"

"We aren't going to have a honeymoon," said Autumn Lea. "Both of us work. Neppie at the shoe factory and I am a nurse's aide at the hospital."

"I will come to see you," I promised. And watched Autumn Lea and Neppie and Neppie's parents drive off and the Leaptrots, crammed into their car, followed. A Ping-Pong paddle with a celluloid ball dangling from an attached rubber string was left behind. I found it and said to Honey Bunch, "I'll see to it it's returned. Wasn't Autumn Lea a lovely bride? I thought Neppie looked a little seedy though."

Preparing to bake a gingerbread, Honey Bunch said she was fond of weddings.

This was an eventful day. That evening my father was called to a house not far from us to pray for a sick grandfather and came home late with a dressed duck and a hamper of pickling cucumbers. Honey Bunch baked the duck successfully but the cucumbers did not turn out well and were finally buried in the back yard. Even then their soured smell leaked out and some curious, night-prowling dogs dug up the stinking mess. Honey Bunch made more racket over this than a road machine. She demanded to know why we always had to live in castaway places and be second-rate citizens. Said she wanted a decent home for us with a fence around it. Cried that she was worn out with having to make one dollar do the work of three. She ordered Daddy to kindly get his nose out of his books and his body out of the house. He was so surprised that he went and stayed all day. It was evening when he returned and Honey Bunch had calmed down. He was discouraged and Honey Bunch was contrite. She blamed it all on the cucumbers. "Next time tell them we prefer corn or greens," she said. "Or another duck."

It was an uneven and suspenseful time. All of us except Elver were aware of it and each of us did his own private share of fretting.

To my sister, brothers, and me, our father and mother showed their worry concerning our future only a little. Our father said, "Now, now. We aren't going to starve or be set out in the street. Your mother and I were a long time in planning for what we're doing now. Go play. If you feel that playing is a waste of time find something constructive to do but keep it simple. People have got to learn to simplify." He put together a tastefully-sized white cross and climbed up to place it on the pointed front of our church-house and spent much time writing and meditating. Honey Bunch kept Elver close to her as she went about her house duties. He loved to wash everything that could be made to shine.

With the money received from pop bottles which they redeemed from ditches, vacant lots, abandoned buildings, construction sites, and the like, Tillie, Hershal, and Barton bought a third-hand pup tent and some flooring and erected a tree house among the branches of a showy tree that stood a hundred feet tall and half a city block removed from The Church of Blessed Hope. Somewhere in their travels they acquired a little henchman named Woodrow Carpenter whose father was a clerk in the post office. Woodrow's big-eyed fancy adorned everything it touched. He had had a lot of old stories read to him and could raise a fiend which didn't know where to stop once Woodrow got going on him. As if he were describing them for the police, Wood-row talked of the great, evil beasts who, according to

Woodrow's almost desperate babblings, lived in the hills surrounding Chinquapin Cove. There was a man living with the beasts who looked and acted much like Robinson Crusoe. Woodrow's fiction was a great engine which never ran out of fuel.

Tillie, Hershal, and Barton allowed Woodrow to become a bosom friend. They invited him to share their playhouse in the tree which soon, mainly due to Woodrow's generosity, was stocked with doodads to amuse and things to eat. These four spent many hours in it talking and loafing, occasionally rousing to take renewed interest in their invention—the church collection plate that would reward generous people and scare stingy ones. This was a shallow glass bowl, painted gilt to make it opaque, with a six-volt, dry cell battery and a complexity of wires and buttons attached to its underside but concealed by puffy rosettes of peach-colored crepe paper.

One afternoon I, returning from a round of social visits in various parts of the town, passed beneath the tree and heard the invention being demonstrated. The voices of my sister, brothers, and Woodrow, joined in the conspiracy, floated down to me. Hershal was being the boss. He was saying, "Awright now, play like we're in church and it's time to take up the money. I'm the deacon so it's my job to pass the plate. I'm standing here in the aisle and you're sitting there listening to the music. I lean in like this, see, past two other people sitting next to you and you put your money in."

"I don't like to give money to churches," said Woodrow. "They don't give you anything back for it. All they do is try and make you think God's going to get you all the time."

"Woodrow," said Tillie. "That's not true. My father doesn't try to make anybody think God is after them. Wait a minute. I just thought about something. If our members tithe, like they do in some churches, then they'll put their money in those little paper envelopes and you won't be able to see how much they drop in the collection plate."

This possibility was ignored. Barton said, "Oh, go ahead, Hershal."

"Tillie," said Hershal. "Here's the plate. I'm holding it in front of you. Put your money in. Okay, you're a good, generous woman so I reward you by ringing this little bell. I push this little button and the bell rings. Isn't that cute? Oh, sholey, this is the sweetest invention I ever thought of."

"Now test the klaxon," said Tillie's voice. "Barton, drop your dime in. No, don't try to take the plate. Hershal's the deacon; he's supposed to hold on to it. Just drop your dime in."

There was a little tinkle, a second of silence, and then the klaxon sounded, a ghostly, vibrant wail, *ahoooooooooga, ahoooooooooga,* that shivered the air and caused the squirrels, playing in a nearby tree, to leap for cover. When it had died away Tillie's satisfied voice said, "It works. We can put it away for now. Let's have some refreshments."

I climbed the arrangement of nailed boards that was the ladder to the tree house and went inside the hot, messy pup tent with my sister, brothers, and Woodrow. The canvas walls of the tent tinged their faces green. "There's some orangeade," said Tillie. "But the ice is all melted. We've been playing. What've you been doing?"

"Visiting some people," I replied. There weren't any sitting conveniences and to stand was impossible because the roof of the tent was so low. I had to squat between Barton and Hershal and the orangeade was too sweet.

"What people?" asked Barton, uncurious. He had blacked out two of his front teeth with Black Jack gum.

I began to tell them of Josie Cullers who was a neighbor to Miss Pearl Drawhorne but not a good one because of Miss Pearl's parrot, Fletcher, who one day went through the Ligustrum hedge that separated Miss Pearl's house from Josie's and snocked off all the heads of Josie's prize amaryllis. And not only that, he then scratched the bulbs from the ground and ate them.

"I kind of like parrots," said Hershal. "But what are amaryllis?"

"They're tall, beautiful lilies," I said, informing them. "Josie's were rose-red and she loved them. They were the only beautiful things in her life. She's a typing clerk in Mr. Merlin Choate's office and is always busier than a one-armed paperhanger and he's always setting the wastebasket on fire with his old cigarette ashes; if anybody else did that he'd fire them. And whenever Josie's sick, like she was today, he sends somebody to her house to find out if she's lying. She wishes she had the stomach to put poison in his coffee. Work, work, work. She says that's all he knows. She loved her lilies and used to come home from work every afternoon and sit beside them. So when she caught Fletcher tearing them up she was madder than a scalded yard-dog and she and Miss Pearl Drawhorne had words and then she phoned the police only they couldn't do anything because Fletcher is just a bird; he can't understand English. So then she and Miss Pearl stopped speaking to each other. Up until this morning they were mortal enemies for ten years."

"Seems like," commented Tillie, "everybody in this town is a mortal enemy to somebody else. Mr. Mast said it was in the air; said the air was bad and needed to be cleared. When I lived with the Masts it seemed like every time I looked out the door there'd be another enemy coming to get Mr. Mast to sue somebody or make some kind of other trouble. Mrs. Mast said people in this town are too much employed."

I thrust my legs out, one by one, to ease the squatter's cramps in them. "Miss Pearl and Josie are coming to our church next Sunday. Together. The most interesting thing; it's like a miracle."

"What zodiac sign is Josie?" inquired Tillie. "Not that I've started believing it makes any difference."

"Josie," I answered, "is a Sagittarius woman. That's a person born between November twenty-third and through December twenty-first. Josie's birth date is the fourteenth of December. Sagittarius people come under the ninth sign of the zodiac which is seen to the astrologist as an archer but sometimes as half-man and half-horse. The symbol for the Archers is a bow and arrow and they have hearts as great as the world. Their pardoning power is glorious but Josie didn't know that until I talked to her about herself this morning."

"Oh, naturally," said Tillie with her fingers on her lips.

"Yes. But before I tell you the rest of this I want to say, you can forget about using that collection plate of yours in church. Just forget it. It's vulgar. Do you want people to think we're vulgar?"

"No," answered Hershal. "We sholey do not want people to think we're vulgar. Do we, Tillie? Do we, Barton?"

"We most sholey do not," said Barton.

"We have breeding, same as you," declared Tillie.

"I also," said Woodrow, solemn as words on a gravestone.

"Please go on with your story," said Tillie courteously. "You say you talked to Josie about herself this morning?"

"Yes. And then we decided to make some candles. Josie has a recipe her grandmother left her but had never tried it. I wanted to put some marbles or something in mine to make it different but we couldn't find anything so I saw Miss Pearl out in her yard and ran out and told her what we were doing and she had a bag of little colored stones she bought for Fletcher only he didn't like them. So she came over and all of us made candles and put the stones in them. So pretty. Josie and Miss Pearl are going to make some big white ones for our church."

"That is totally the most interesting thing I ever heard," said Tillie. "But kind of spooky. That could never have happened to anybody but you, Delpha."

I pulled two long swatches of my hair forward and tied them together under my chin. "No, it could have happened to anybody. Then I went to see the Leaptrots. Mr. Leaptrot is the night watchman at the shoe factory and knows just everybody so I thought he could just mention our church to . . . What I mean to say is there are so many in his family. Mrs. Leaptrot says she has to count them twice a day to be sure nobody's missing. They're never all together so I thought it would be nice if they could all come to worship with us on Sundays and sit together and be friends and rejoice with us. Their cat got killed last week. Mrs. Leaptrot says she's sure it was Bumper Choate who ran over it. He goes looking for cats to kill, she says. She says Bumper's got no business being the sheriff; that if it wasn't for his daddy he'd have drowned a long time ago 'cause he hasn't got enough sense to come in out of a shower of rain. Four of her children are Libras and she's one too. Their sign is Scales and they believe in adventure and justice. The whole Leaptrot family is going to come to our church next Sunday and bring their friends."

Hershal and Barton, with their heads lain on their up-drawn knees, appeared to have fallen asleep and Tillie had her eyes closed. Woodrow alone remained attentive. The wind was gently rocking the tree house.

CANCER

THE CRAB

JUNE 22ND THROUGH JULY 23RD

Lunar inconstancy bathed in the
Moonlight of pessimistic optimism.

FIVE

There was a man in Chinquapin Cove by the name of Judge Tate Potter and it was said of him that his credentials were not quite proper for the title of Justice of the Peace. Josie Cullers and Miss Pearl Drawhorne were both in the possession of a lot of information about him. Josie said he had been a high-stepping rascal in Savannah, Georgia, and New Orleans, Louisiana; a real dandy with the ladies and not very true to the laws of the legal profession. Miss Pearl said she had never known anybody who could spout the phrases of the law as skillfully as the judge. With the assistance of Sheriff Bumper Choate he kept the peace of the town and sometimes Bumper took violators to his house in the middle of the night and so well did he know his job he could hear the cases and dispose of them without leaving his bed. Miss Pearl and Josie too laughed like loons when telling their stories about the judge. They asked me to imagine him in pajamas, dealing with a culprit in the dead of night in this language: *"Sic utere tuo ut alienum non laedas,"* meaning owners of land lying on the bank of a stream could make use of the water but could not dam it up. And: *"Lex non cogit ad impossibilia,"* meaning the law never required impossibilities.

I never saw anything but the quiet style of Judge Potter. That is the way he went about his business. His office was in a downtown building next door to that of Sheriff Bumper Choate and he lived alone in a red brick house and three times a week a woman who was uglier than homemade sin and was a gunnysack of gloom, went to clean for him. According to my friends, he owned some silver pieces of handmade tableware which he claimed to be properties inherited from ancestors who had explored Florida years before any of the English colonies settled in the New World. He was writing a history of himself and his ancestors and, though an aging man with occasional sufferings of the shakes and other inconsequential ailments, jumped like a cold drop of water on a hot griddle whenever Mr. Merlin Choate snapped his fingers.

One Sunday, about six weeks after the inauguration of The Church of Blessed Hope, Judge Potter, fittingly attired in a white linen suit and a soft, cream-colored hat, appeared at our church-house and was an interested spectator to the morning service which was unusually gracious and inspiring. There might have been fifty people there not counting us Greens. White candles in gleaming, graduated sizes and vases of summer flowers had been set about. Our church now owned an old upright piano which had been salvaged from Josie Cullers' basement. Honey Bunch played it.

Axe Aleywine and Betty Jean Swain arrived together and sat as close to each other as the occasion would allow. Miss Pearl Drawhorne, Axe's mother, and Josie Cullers sat across the aisle. Fletcher sat on Miss Pearl's knee and occasionally his laugh, so weirdly like Miss Pearl's, would cause my father to pause in his sermon and smile and everybody else smiled too. My father spoke to these people in a real, simple way and they, because they were tired of their lives the way they were and here was a man of God who spoke like no other man of God they had ever heard before, leaned forward and listened. They nodded and forgot themselves and murmured, "That's right." Air stirring in the church was fresh because all of the windows were wide open. This was the picture.

At offering time my dad sat down and folded his hands and meditated and Honey Bunch played suitable music. Hershal passed the collection plate he had invented and the little bell tinkled for the generous ones and the klaxon sounded *ahoooooooooooga, ahoooooooooooga* for the stingy ones and appropriately the people either laughed or nearly jumped out of their skins. Betty Jean Swain got the klaxon and her scream went to the ceiling and Fletcher, dancing around on Miss Pearl's knee, fluttered his feathers and screamed, "Oh, you're a caution! Bless Pat! By jingo!"

My father came down from his speaker's platform quicker than I'd ever seen him move and rushed down the aisle toward Hershal but Axe Aleywine's mother, with her little lace hat slightly askew over one eye and her handkerchief pressed to her forehead, stepped out to stop him, saying, "Now, Reverend, what harm? What harm. You were a boy once yourself and it's a good show. God might even be on the side of it, how do you know He's not? Didn't you just get through telling us one of the motives of God was to free us of our dull imaginations so we could have some fun?"

"Oh, you're a caution!" cried Fletcher.

"I don't know what to say," said my dad, appealing to the congregation. "I believe imagination is the most principal source of human improvement and I encourage my children to be inventive—"

"Oh," said Miss Pearl Drawhorne. "Everybody here knows this isn't a run-of-the-mill church, Reverend. That's why we came. We've all enjoyed ourselves for a change, even Fletcher here. I ask you, what other church would be so liberal as to let me bring my bird to services?"

"By jingo!" said Fletcher, examining his scaly feet and Honey Bunch, who had stopped her music, started playing again and Hershal finished taking the offering but didn't ring the bell or make the klaxon sound again. Then the congregation sang again, my father said the benediction and the service for that Sunday morning was over.

Judge Potter allowed everyone to precede him from this meeting. My father stood at the door of our church-house, shaking hands with the people, smiling with them and chatting and accepting their promises to return. Judge Potter waited until the last one had gone before saying what he had come to say. The nature of this did not long remain a secret because among us almost everything is common property. At the noon dinner table my father said, "Judge Potter tells me this building is to be razed."

Honey Bunch almost dropped the gravy. "Razed! You mean demolished? Torn down? But that can't be! It belongs to Mrs. Merlin Choate. We're renting it from her."

"Daddy," said Tillie. "May I have the gizzard if nobody else asks for it?"

"I am sorry about the collection plate," said Hershal. "I understand I have to be punished for it. Tillie and Barton too. Delpha didn't have anything to do with it. We won't ever use it in church again; we promise."

"I was embarrassed," said Barton. "I never thought people would laugh at it."

With a serving fork my father lifted the gizzard from the platter of fried chicken in front of his own plate and laid it on Tillie's. "The judge said Mrs. Choate is mentally unbalanced and not responsible for her actions. I told him I'd come to his office tomorrow morning."

Honey Bunch was settling Elver in his high chair, tying his bib around his neck, placing his food and eating utensils on his tray. After a moment she said, "There aren't any more places for rent in this town. The children and I looked before we found this one. It's a trick of some kind."

My father tried to cover his distress. In a fuzzy way he said, "A trick?"

"Maybe trick is not the word," said Honey Bunch,

displaying some anger. "Maybe I should have said it's a maneuver."

"I will go see Judge Potter tomorrow morning," said my father.

"You are never able to see the bad side of people," said Honey Bunch.

"You are mistaken about that," said my father, quietly reproving.

"I'm sorry," said Honey Bunch, so distressed. "I shouldn't have said that. It's just that we've seen so much of the bad sides of people. It's just that there doesn't seem to be any end to it. The judge won't say anything more to you tomorrow morning than he's already said. He only repeats what he is told to say. I think it's a waste of time for you to go to his office. We'll have to move, that's all."

"Again," said Barton, dismayed. Hershal had forgotten his hunger. He was pouring too much sugar in his iced tea. Tillie, the extremely sensitive and deeply sympathetic little Crab child, had snatched up her gizzard and was gnawing it villainously. But then, remembering, she dropped it back in her plate as if it were a live coal. Desolate, she said, "We haven't said grace."

"I will say it," I said. "Everybody bow his head. Oh, God, we give thanks for this food we are about to receive. We pray that on this day and every other day both our friends and enemies shall not be hungry. If our enemies hunger we pray they will be fed and if they be thirsty we pray they will drink. Please bless all of us here and everybody. Amen."

Tillie and I always did the Sunday dishes. I washed and

she wiped and during the performance of this chore she said she thought it wasn't very bright of me to pray that our enemies shouldn't go hungry or thirsty. She wanted to know if that part of my meal-prayer had been sincere.

I said, "While I was saying it, it was sincere. I thought it sounded nice, especially since it's Sunday."

"How about now?" she asked.

I said, "Now I've changed my mind. I don't think I care if our enemies are hungry or thirsty. I am thinking. I am thinking."

"About what?"

"Sugar," I said.

"Sugar?"

"It catches more flies than vinegar."

"Oh, my conscience."

"And cats."

"Cats?"

"There is more than one way to skin one," I said. "Our parents always say so and they are right. They are right about the sugar and vinegar too."

SCORPIO
THE SCORPION
OCTOBER 24TH THROUGH NOVEMBER 22ND

Proud eagle, gray lizard or stinging scorpion.
The Phoenix rises from nuclear Pluto.

SIX

Some people do not respond to others and Judge Tate Potter was one of them. I think he might have been one of those adults who regard all children with distaste and a chilling expression. He was the kind to accept compliments as if they were his due. On Monday afternoon I described my first and only person-to-person encounter with this person: "I told him I was there in his office for an educational reason—that's why Daddy let me go with him this morning—and the judge said, 'Don't touch anything. Sit over there and be quiet.' I told him he made me think of Cupid. He did too because he's little and fat. Then I looked closer and saw

I might have made a mistake but by that time it was too late."

"I have never," said Miss Pearl, "associated Judge Potter's image with that of Cupid. I just can't call to my mind any picture of the judge running around shooting arrows into people making them fall in love." She was grating the meat from a fresh coconut, preparing to make macaroons. "But your educational reason for visiting the judge's office this morning," she said. "You didn't tell me that."

I was having a slice of Miss Pearl's freshly baked bread spread with butter and jelly. I offered a morsel to Fletcher who refused it, preferring the slivers of coconut which occasionally flew from Miss Pearl's grater to the floor. He stood beneath her work table and from time to time made a meaningless contribution to the conversation taking place.

"I wanted to see what a judge's office looked like," said I. "Maybe I'll be one myself someday. I don't know though; they're kind of creepy. Judge Potter is."

"Indeed he is that," agreed Miss Pearl. "Sometimes when I take Fletcher out for his evening walk we go past his house and I tell you it gives me a real chill just to look in through his windows and see him all hunched over those crazy papers he's always writing and when I look at him I think I'm looking at the devil's advocate and it wouldn't surprise me a bit to see fire spurt from his mouth sometimes."

"I wish people wouldn't use words on me I haven't learned yet," I said. "Just because I don't look like a child—"

"The devil's advocate is a person who always sides in with the devil," explained Miss Pearl. "Usually because either he hasn't got sense enough to have a side of his own or because he knows which side his bread is buttered on and doesn't want it taken away from him. It's too bad about Judge Potter, the way he kowtows to Merlin Choate. Still, you have to look at his side of it too; he isn't any spring chicken anymore and where would he go if he had to leave Chinquapin Cove? I am positive he couldn't hold office anywhere else. But you started to tell me what happened in his office this morning."

I took a bite of my jelly bread. "Judge Potter said to Daddy that the church-house we're living in now is going to be torn down and we'd have to move. Daddy said move where and the judge said he didn't know. Daddy said there weren't any more places to rent in Chinquapin Cove and the judge said he couldn't help that. Said maybe we should go to another town."

"Oh," said Miss Pearl and pulled a chair out from the table and sat in it. Fletcher waddled out from underneath the table and she picked him up, holding him in her aproned lap and stroking his head. After a while she said, "Well, maybe your father could build a house of his own."

"Yes," I said.

"Except that it would take an awful lot of money."

"An awful lot."

"And I don't know where he'd get the land to put it on. There isn't any for sale in Chinquapin Cove."

I considered Miss Pearl and the soppy feeling of frustration that was flopping around in my stomach. "I might go to see Mr. Choate."

Miss Pearl said, "No. This isn't a child's game. You shouldn't even be concerned with any of it. I can't think why your father is letting you be."

"It was an accident," I said, lowering my stiff white lashes to half mast and gazing through them at Miss Pearl. "I went with Daddy this morning to Judge Potter's office for education purposes. What would Mr. Merlin Choate do to me if I went to see him? Eat me?"

Miss Pearl had turned all of her attention to Fletcher, had her head bent to his, was exchanging looks with him. She fed him coconut from the bowl of slivers on the table. "Merlin is in the hospital," she said. "He's taken a room there and is resting. Josie said he wasn't seeing anybody."

Referring to Purple Bubble Gum, I said, "A girl I know told me that when Mr. Merlin Choate doesn't want anybody to live in this town he puts the skids to them. She said one time a man named Mr. Lake come down here from up north and wrote a lot of stuff about Mr. Choate and Judge Potter and Bumper Choate. He was going to put it in a magazine but Mr. Choate found out about it and hired three men to make him change his mind. They burned up all of Mr. Lake's papers and made him leave Chinquapin Cove. My friend says that is what happens to everybody Mr. Merlin Choate doesn't like. He just hires people to make them leave. That's why this town is so little and why nobody new hardly ever comes."

"If I were you I shouldn't concern myself with anyone like Merlin Choate," said Miss Pearl, closing this conversation. "Nobody has ever got the better of him. I can vouch for that."

The hospital at Chinquapin Cove was contained in a two-story building on a street named Zinnia and was the ugly color of liver. Its windows and doors were faulty and its settled pillars had long ago given up trying to evenly support the weight of its floors. There was a porch of once-white concrete studded with tan river stones and eight steps to climb which were not proportioned to each other. On both sides of these there was a mass of leafage into which patients dropped Band-Aids, tissues, toothpicks, and sometimes tears. Actually it was more a place for the very old and for those whose diseases had been a part of them for a long time, though it did have an operating room with passable lighting. It had only two elevators and not enough employees. Dr. Elspeth, the surgeon of Chinquapin Cove, was the one in charge of this business. When first I saw him, I thought he was an ugly man but later this feeling changed because he was so kind and was short-tempered only when he saw his patients being neglected. The nurses did not dare to remind him what they were or were not supposed to do according to the rules of their profession. The nurses' aides were terrified of him; they were required to do kitchen duty whenever there was a shortage of culinary help.

On the day I paid my first visit to the hospital Autumn Lea Nation had been assigned the task of peeling potatoes and scraping carrots. It was three o'clock in the afternoon and she was the only person in the kitchen. She had been crying and didn't act at all glad to see me.

"I had a time finding you," I said, hopping down the dim steps that connected an upper hallway to this room. "Been all over this place looking and nobody knew where you were. A lady showed me some cookies she keeps under her mattress. She said you might have gone home."

"I should but I can't," said Autumn Lea and threw a skinned potato into a tub containing water and other skinned potatoes. "What are you doing here?"

"Oh," I answered, "I was just passing by and thought I'd drop in a minute and see how you were getting along. How's Neppie?"

Autumn Lea speared another potato from the basket at her elbow and viciously started to hack away its skin. "He's fine. I'm not though. For two cents I'd quit this job and go to work in the dime store except they're not putting on any new help right now. I hate this place worse than dirt. If somebody told you to take a man who wasn't unconscious up to surgery what would you do?"

"If I was working in a hospital I guess I'd do it," I said. "What's surgery?"

"That's the room where Dr. Elspeth operates on people," said Autumn Lea. A tear slid out of one eye and down her peaches-and-cream cheek. "The nurses' aides aren't allowed to go in there except to do the clean-up work. We've got germs. We're the stupidest people ever lived, so don't know whether we're afoot or on horseback unless somebody tells us. That's what the Queen of the May says about us. She thinks just because she's a registered nurse she's got large brains, but I can assure you they aren't the size of a pea."

"I wouldn't want to be a nurse," I said. "I've been thinking about becoming an explorer. You ever wondered what the top of the world looks like?"

"No," answered Autumn Lea. "Why should I? I live at the bottom. The May Queen is jealous of me because I've got Neppie and she can't find a husband because she's such an old fish. She just can't find enough dirty work for me to do and the way she gives orders nobody can understand her. This morning she told me to take a patient up to surgery and I did and she got mad. She didn't tell me *how* to take him up. Just said, 'Nation, take this man up to surgery, I'll meet you there.' She calls everybody by their last name."

"So how'd you take him up?" I inquired.

"Why," said Autumn Lea, "I walked him up the stairs. There wasn't anything much wrong with him. He was just going to have his appendix taken out. Looked fine to me. Said he felt all right. He'd only had one little shot to make him groggy and still knew what he was doing. So I took him up the stairs to surgery and the Queen of the May met us at the door and almost had a heart attack. Said I should have put him on a roller-stretcher and taken him up in the elevator. Dr. Elspeth screamed when Queenie opened the door and he saw me and the patient. I never heard such a fuss over nothing."

I was looking around for something to sit on. Every stool and chair was occupied with something related to kitchenry; bundled towels and loose ones and stacks of washed and unwashed pots and pans. There had been an accident of some sort with the dishwashing machine. It stood in a puddle and was steaming and its sides and front were covered with several inches of still, white foam. "I didn't know you had to use a special kind of soap in it," explained Autumn Lea. "Queenie just told me to load it up and get it going so that's what I did. She was down here just a minute ago and said I'd put the wrong kind of soap in it. How could I know, I've never operated a dishwasher. *Can't* you find a place to sit down? Well, move something, for pity's sake. Want to help me peel some potatoes? It's not my job but we don't have any kitchen help today, they all quit and I don't blame them. Here's a knife, you don't have to be particular. I've eaten tons of potato skins during my life and they haven't killed me yet."

I sat on a high stool at the kitchen work table and helped Autumn Lea peel potatoes. In spite of its muss and disorganization this kitchen was rather pleasant. Its walls were painted light gray and its floors were bleached from many years of scrubbings. Its windows were clean and bare and looked out to a kind of little courtyard where scarlet bougainvillea bloomed and a trickle from a spigot sparkled in the brightness of the afternoon.

Autumn Lea was the kind of conversationalist that could talk about six subjects all at once. "That lady with the cookies under her mattress, that's Mrs. Quisenberry. She's an alcoholic from watching television, her son told me; that's what she's in here getting treated for. He's suing the television people for what they did to his mother. When his father died he got her a television set so she wouldn't be lonely and every time advertising would come on she'd get up and go in her room and have a little drink. We're going to have beef stew for supper tonight, that's what the potatoes are for. I hate it. I don't know who's going to make it, maybe I'll get to do it. Nobody'll eat, the patients just pick

76

at their food. Neppie has decided he wants to do something creative with his life now. There's a side to him he didn't know about until just recently. There's quite a bit of trouble at the shoe factory now because everybody's got it in his mind all of a sudden he wants to do something besides just work all the time. Axe Aleywine and Mr. Choate had a big argument one day last week because now Axe only wants to work two days a week. Because he's a foreman Mr. Choate says he has got to work six. He's got a big rock in his yard and is making a statue of Theodore Roosevelt out of it. Neppie and I are thinking about leaving here and going to Tennessee. His grandfather lives up there; makes his living whittling birds and animals. That's what Neppie wants to do."

"Do you know what room Mr. Merlin Choate is in?" I asked, slinging my finished potato into the tub of water and taking up another.

"Sure," answered Autumn Lea. "He isn't sick; he's just resting but you'd think he was crippled the way he has to be waited on. Neppie learned how to whittle from his grandfather when he was just a little kid. Last night when we got home from church he whittled the most beautiful pheasant; you should see it."

"What room is Mr. Merlin Choate in?"

"Thirty-eight. I am thinking about quitting this job as soon as I get these potatoes peeled. Queenie has got me mad now. Neppie and I need the money though if we're going to move to Tennessee. I don't know what you want to see Mr. Merlin Choate for, he's the meanest man God ever let breathe. Be careful if you go to see him, he throws things."

"Oh," I said. "Mr. Merlin Choate does not scare me. He is just a Scorpio. That is his trouble, I think."

"A Scorpio," said Autumn Lea, irritated. "You talk so peculiar, everybody says so. You make me nervous. Your eyes are so peculiar, why don't you wear sunglasses?"

I said, "I am not talking peculiar, Autumn Lea. You are just understanding peculiar. In the science of astrology of which I became a student last year, Scorpio is a person born on October twenty-fourth through November twenty-second. If I had my pick, to try and shoe a goose or get next to a Scorpio, I'd pick the goose but they are here just like everybody else so there is nothing to be done except try to understand them. They are tricky but have their nice, good sides just like other people. Scorpios always have to go around looking on the worst side of things because they think everybody is trying to cheat them and they have to act like they are evil because they are a teensy bit afraid all the time somebody will catch them by the tail and look at them through a magnifying glass and see they are not pure poison."

"After I get these potatoes peeled I have to scrape carrots," said Autumn Lea. "Thank your stars you don't work here." She slung another denuded potato into the tub so hard it caused a little spout to rise and splash out.

Trying to act like a carefree child because the vague, careless behavior of children is always more quickly pardoned, I went hop, hopping back up the dim stairs to the floor over the kitchen and wandered down two corridors until I stood in front of room thirty-eight. Its door was closed and there weren't any sounds coming from it. All of the corridor was silent and closed.

During the time it had taken me to come from Miss Pearl's house to the hospital I had gotten hold of myself so that now again I was completely in charge of myself and I was in charge of this mission of mine too. Decision tasted fresh and crisp in my mouth. I was Delpha Green, a Water Bearer, favored by the airy sign of Aquarius, as light and carefree as a breeze-blown rose petal. My feet were as weightless as dandelion down and my heart, thump-thumping, silky inside me, was considerate, skipping just a small beat every now and then. Mr. Merlin Choate would be pleased to have me for his visitor and why shouldn't he be? He couldn't be any different than others I had known. Probably he was bored with his life of lonely power and was just waiting for somebody like me to come along so he could confide his troubles and fears. Probably nobody had ever thought to ask him if he had troubles and fears and after I had heard them and, in turn, talked to him a bit about my own concerns . . . Well, it was very possible that he and I could then, at least, reach some kind of understanding whereby he could be made to see there were other citizens in the town with their rights too and if they behaved in a reasonable way why couldn't he also?

I raised my clenched hand and rapped on Mr. Merlin Choate's door and his voice came so quick and so loud I jumped. It made my inner ears quiver, it was so harsh. It was precisely what I had expected and when I pushed the door open and looked in and saw him complete against his pillows I wasn't a bit surprised. His head was pointed like a scorpion's.

79

LEO

THE LION

JULY 24TH THROUGH AUGUST 23RD

*Transparent vulnerabilities descending
On rays of the roaring Sun.*

SEVEN

The person of Mr. Merlin Choate could be generally described as being the color of old straw even to his large, unblinking eyes and his hair which grew in a low, encircling fringe. His flesh stretched over his inelegant bones in short supply. Really he looked quite a bit like a cornfield scarecrow and all during my short visit with him I kept half expecting to see him spring from his bed and stand outstretched like one. He was the kind of person who commanded a certain formality.

"Good afternoon," I said, going up to within three feet of his bed and stopping beside a chair. "My name is Delpha

Green and I am here visiting friends and just now when I passed your door I thought I heard you call. Did you call?"

"No," answered Mr. Merlin Choate. "I did not." Under the sheet which covered him loosely he appeared to be decently clothed in hospital pajamas. He was not going to respond to me and the thought slid through my mind that he had never responded to any simple friendliness. His face had no real expression; it looked as if it had never experienced one. His ears curled close to his head and were too small for his face; he had not one redeeming feature. He was as ugly as his reputation and wasn't liking this intrusion and was only going to tolerate it for a minute.

Words that I hadn't thought to rehearse rattled from my mouth. "Oh, excuse me then. My, what a pretty room. It's cooler than the others, isn't it? And much nicer. Are you comfortable? Is it possible you need something? I could get it for you since I'm here. It must be terrible to be bedridden. Would you like me to get you a pitcher of fresh water or do you need an errand performed? There is a drugstore half a block from here. Do you need a headache powder or cough drops or anything like that? Perhaps a magazine? Razor blades?"

"I am not bedridden," said Mr. Merlin Choate. "I have everything I need. Everything." He regarded me as if I were a stick of furniture.

Because I sensed I was about to be invited to leave, I skipped quickly around to the front of the chair and plopped myself down in it. "I was just down in the kitchen helping Autumn Lea Nation peel potatoes. She is a nurse's aide here. Guess what you're going to have for your supper to-night. Beef stew."

Mr. Merlin Choate's gaze was steady and almost alarmingly intense.

"Autumn Lea's husband works in your shoe factory," I said.

"Don't you think I know that?" said Merlin Choate.

"But he wants to be a wood carver like his grandfather. Last night when he got home from my father's church he carved the most beautiful pheasant. This is a queer hospital, I think. Maybe I shouldn't say that though because it is the only one I have ever been in so I don't know how others are. I don't even think I was born in a hospital. Seems to me I can remember the day I was born. My father wasn't a minister then; he had some other kind of a job. It was very cold because I was born on the twenty-fifth of January and there was frost on all the windows and my father stuck a new penny on one of them for good luck. He is a kind, beautiful man believing God lives in the hearts of people and they should look for Him there. He says people don't look hard enough for God in their hearts and that is why they are separated from Him. He says people should stop feeling guilty about God and stop fearing Him and learn to hope more and have some fun. I told my father I thought if people could understand themselves they could find God quicker. I am a student of astrology."

"You should learn to stop for air once in a while," said Mr. Merlin Choate, dry as a summer seed and restless. It wasn't likely he would remain where he was for long.

Headlong and with an awful kind of clumsiness, I plunged on. There was such a total lack of human expression in Merlin Choate's face I couldn't think he had ever been a father, tolerant to the babblings of a child, although there was his son, Bumper Choate, the sheriff of Chinquapin Cove; no one could deny his presence. I tied my hair under my chin and grinned and said, "Somebody told me the date of your birth and I've been reading about you in one of my astrology books. Do you know what your zodiac sign is? It's Scorpio. You're a Scorpion and people who don't understand you think all you do is run around poisoning people but I don't think that's true. I think you only sting people when you are trying to make them behave themselves. Everybody should behave themselves, that is what my father says in his sermons every Sunday and if it takes a little sting every now and then, well, I am sure it doesn't hurt too much."

"It's nice of you to be concerned about the reasons for my deportment," said Mr. Merlin Choate, "but believe me I don't need anybody to make excuses for it."

"Astrology is an old, old art," I said. "Or science, whichever one you want to call it. I prefer to call it art. Some say it's just superstition and they might be right, to think the sun, moon, planets, and stars have anything to do with the way people are. I don't know. All I know is it helps me understand myself and other people too. When you understand people you don't mind their faults so much; it's easier to love them. Probably you would be surprised to know how easy it is to understand people according to their zodiac signs. Yourself, for instance. Being a Scorpion you are ruled by the planet Pluto so you have passions in you which don't let you rest. You are intelligent and love to work and when other people get in the way of your work it makes you so mad and then you start to throw yourself around—like this, see? You make more noise than a skeleton having a fit on a hardwood floor. Like this, see?" In this moment of madness, in a sudden, wild effort to bring from Mr. Merlin Choate some display of feeling—anything would do—I slipped from my chair and pretended to be a skeleton having a fit on the hardwood floor.

"What in the name of curiosity!" exclaimed Mr. Merlin Choate, jerking upright in his bed.

Heaving and flailing and kicking my heels, I became quite carried away with my own performance. At least it was getting the attention it deserved. I clacked my teeth a couple of times and remembered to beat my forehead with my fist.

"Get up!" said Mr. Merlin Choate. "Get up off that floor!"

Again I sat in the chair and tried to breathe normally. "Excuse me. I got carried away, I guess. I was just telling you about yourself. I don't mean to say you ever act like that but some Scorpios do because they're lonely and want attention. I feel sorry for them."

"You don't need to feel sorry for me," said Mr. Merlin Choate. "I have never been lonely."

"Scorpios love beauty," I said, losing ground. "When it's summer like it is now—"

"I don't have time for summer," said Mr. Merlin Choate coming out from under his sheet to reach for his robe which lay in a crumble across the foot of his bed. "And I don't believe in astrology. To me it's a lot of tripe."

"Tripe, sir?"

"Tripe. Hot air. Hooey."

"Oh, hooey," I said and laughed. I hadn't the vaguest idea what tripe was or hooey either. By this time Mr. Merlin Choate had his robe on over his pajamas and was fishing in his bedside glass for his teeth. He lifted them dripping and in one practiced motion inserted them in his mouth, seating them against his gums with his tongue. He didn't apologize for this bit of crudity. He was going through the pockets of his robe to find his spectacles, to set them on his face, and he was the cunning little lizard who had out-streaked everybody, not ever being lonely, living in the world all this time but not having time for one of the world's simple, beautiful pleasures—summer. Not time for a smile even; probably he had never had that. Probably he had never trusted the world but had always had the thought in his mind just to bully it and make it cower to him.

Properly attired according to the place where he was, Mr. Merlin Choate was going out to buy a newspaper and he didn't say excuse me or it was nice of you to stop in and see me, come back again or anything like that. Just said, "Going down to the lobby for a newspaper."

I stood and watched him go toward the door and open it. "Mr. Merlin Choate, sir?"

He turned. Finally he blinked. "What is it?"

"I came here to your room to ask you a question, sir."

"So ask it," said Mr. Merlin Choate.

"My father's church," I said. "You own it and Judge Potter said you were going to tear it down."

"I don't know anything about that," said Mr. Merlin Choate quickly, too quickly.

"My father is the Reverend Green, sir, of The Church of Blessed Hope. He is renting your building and if you tear it down he won't have any place to preach. We live in the back half of it."

"I don't know anything about it," said Mr. Merlin Choate. "My wife must've rented it to your father."

"Yes, sir, she did. And there aren't anymore places to rent in Chinquapin Cove. If you tear it down—"

"Tell your father he should go see Judge Potter," said Mr. Merlin Choate. "He handles my properties; I don't know anything about them."

And that was the stark end of that and no use to shed even one tear over it or lose temper and hurl myself at him and bite him in the leg. Or take the pair of little fingernail scissors from the tray on his nightstand and make short pants out of the long ones which hung sloppily from a doorknob.

I saw Mrs. Quisenberry again and as it turned out my visit with this sprite, rare one was important and decisive. With a finger to her raspberry-colored lips, Mrs. Quisenberry beckoned to me as I passed in the hallway and I went into her room and accepted some broken cookies which had had all the raisins picked out of them.

"Since I gave up drinking I have a constant craving to eat all the time," said Mrs. Quisenberry who was one of the most perfectly pretty people I had ever seen. Her yellow hair was a work of hairdressing art, tucked on the sides and in the back with bright butterfly bows and she had soft, dove-colored eyes. "I've gained ten pounds since I've been here," she said. "Not that the food is anything to write home about; they cook it and throw it out. Nobody eats. I told my friends not to bring me flowers. They bring me food. All I do is eat and sleep. I'm so bored I could spit. How was your visit with Merlin Choate?"

"Terrible," I said.

"Let's sit by the window where it's cooler," said Mrs. Quisenberry and pushed two chairs over. The tiny silver bells dangling from her ear lobes tinkled. "If you were visiting me in my home I would offer you a glass of wine," she said. "Last summer I made forty-five quarts of dandelion and ten of raisin. On a winter night nothing warms the heart any better. It's nice company when you live alone. Better than nothing, anyway. It eases the boredom and helps me sleep. My son and his wife can't understand that; they're such dullards. Total teetotalers, both of them. They can't understand me and I can't understand them. Their house is so clean you can't imagine; I have to take off my shoes when I go see them and their children are so good I wonder if they're bright. How was your visit with Merlin Choate?"

"Terrible," I said again. "I don't like him. He has never been lonely and doesn't have time for summer."

"He is a scoundrel, no question about it," said Mrs. Quisenberry. "I haven't spoken to him since the day of my husband's funeral two years ago and then it was only to ask him to kindly move his car where he had parked it in the driveway of the funeral home so nobody else could get either in or out. I had to get out of my car to do it and it was raining and I got soaked to the skin and almost had pneumonia afterward."

"He is going to tear down our church-house," I said. "I asked him why and he said he didn't know anything about it. He is a rude man and very ugly. No wonder everybody hates him."

"Ha," said Mrs. Quisenberry, finding a stray raisin and popping it into her mouth. "They have better reasons than his ugly face to hate him. You should ask me if you want to know why he's going to tear down your church-house. I can tell you. It's because your father has started everybody in this town thinking there might be something beyond the hills where the crows live or even right here for that matter if they could just wake up. Axe Aleywine's mother was to see me yesterday and she said Axe told her people at the shoe factory are getting up a petition to try and make Merlin Choate shorten the work week at the factory. They're beginning to think there might be something to life besides just working themselves silly for money and a trip to church on Sunday to hear the preacher tell them how guilty they are for things that happened long before they were even thought of. They're tired of feeling guilty; they want to feel hope and love and most of them are blaming Merlin Choate for all of their wasted years. That's why Merlin is going to tear down your church-house. Your father is rocking the boat and Merlin is not liking it."

"In Chinquapin Cove there aren't any other places to rent," I said. "My father and mother are worried. Maybe we'll have to go to another town."

"That would be our loss I am sure," murmured Mrs. Quisenberry. "Pearl Drawhorne and Josie Cullers were both to see me last evening. They say your father delivers a very stirring sermon. Is he an astrologer as well as a minister?"

"No, ma'am. I'm the astrologer. That is, I am a student of astrology."

"Really," said Mrs. Quisenberry and her southern voice was like cream.

"Yes."

"My birthday is the twelfth of August," said Mrs. Quisenberry and her lips tilted to a saucy smile.

"Then you are a Lion," I said. "Your sign is Leo and you are ruled by the sun. Leo ladies are always lovely if not on the outside then on the inside but usually both. Lions love to be grand; they like to get all dressed up and go to parties and dance but they like to have jobs too and be the bosses. When they are bored they are dangerous."

"I am so bored I could spit," said Mrs. Quisenberry. "Last night Pearl and Josie were lit up like a pair of Christmas trees. Josie's got the notion she's going to quit her job at the shoe factory and she and Pearl are going to start up a cosmetic business of their own. I've been thinking I might draw out some of my savings and go in with them. Josie's got a whole shoebox full of wonderful recipes she inherited from her grandparents. She and Pearl are going to make cucumber face cream and honey hand lotion and neck tighteners for women with wrinkled throats and, oh, I don't know what all. They are going to name their line Exotica. Isn't that exciting? Doesn't that excite your mind? They are going to advertise in some of the cheaper, little magazines and do a mail-order business. If you looked in a magazine and saw an advertisement for Exotica Wrinkle Cream would you order a jar? If you had wrinkles?"

"No," I replied.

"Why not?"

"Because it makes me think of Egypt and when I think of Egypt I think of Moses in the bulrushes. I thought it was cruel for him to be put there even if he did get rescued. If I had some wrinkle cream for sale I'd name it after a flower. Bridal wreath or tea rose. No, I think honeysuckle. Everybody loves honeysuckle. It even tastes good. I'd name it honeysuckle."

Mrs. Quisenberry was a very quick person; it was easy to see that she lived an intense life of her own. "I think you're right," she said. "Egypt is a depressing country; all those mummies. Honeysuckle suggests freshness. We're going to make a wrinkle cream and a tonic for flabby skin and one for acne and a shampoo and a tonic hair grower . . . Josie has a whole shoebox of recipes. Pearl is going to design the containers. Each jar and bottle will have a hand painted flower on it. She wants to write verses to go along with each sale but really she can't. Her poetry is dreadful."

"Poetry isn't hard to write," I said. "I do it all the time. For instance, if I was going to write one about you I'd write something like this:

> Lovely Lion lady
> So bored she could spit.
> There are better things.
> Don't sit."

91

Mrs. Quisenberry had both hands up to her cheeks. "Yes," she said. "Yes. Really you're a clever child. You're so strange."

"I have to go now," I said, and it was then Mrs. Quisenberry turned this meeting into an important, decisive one, taking a roundabout way to say she had known Merlin Choate for almost all of his nasty, greedy life and wouldn't she just like to be the one to put the skids under him or at least supply the grease. She owned two Quonset huts, inherited from her dear, departed husband, which stood on an acre of ground five minutes from the center of town, fifteen if you had to walk it, and wouldn't it be just the ticket for the Honeysuckle Cosmetic Company to occupy one and the Greens the other. They were insulated and equipped with modern plumbing facilities. In the last year of his life her husband had planned to set up a cabinet-making business in them, instead he had dropped dead at his desk in Merlin Choate's office one afternoon.

Mrs. Quisenberry had a personality that was positively electrifying. She was the kind to put thoughts in people's heads they'd never had before. One time a stranger stopped at her door just to ask directions but Mrs. Quisenberry engaged him in a thirty-minute conversation concerning politics and got him so worked up over the state of national affairs that afterward he rushed to the nearest public telephone and called the President of the United States.

That's the kind of person Mrs. Quisenberry was.

TAURUS
THE BULL
APRIL 21ST THROUGH MAY 21ST

Really real and hurrying
Slowly with Venus by the hand.

EIGHT

Better times then befell my family and me. One day soon after my hospital visit with Mrs. Quisenberry we moved to the larger of her two Quonset huts which, true to her description, sat side by side smack in the center of an acre of wooded, grassy land five minutes from the center of the town, fifteen if you had to walk it. A live creek, spawning from a spring bubbling upward beneath the trees on the north corner of this place, slid through it.

Axe Aleywine, Neppie Nation, and Mr. Leaptrot came in a truck and moved the piano and all the other church trappings. It was Neppie who crawled up and pried the white cross from the front of Mr. Merlin Choate's building. Tillie, Hershal, and Barton dismantled their tree house and Mr. Leaptrot, who had placed himself in charge of the moving operation, backed the truck down the block and loaded it all. In its unjoined, collapsed state it was rather a pitiful sight. There was an empty hornets' nest on the underside of one of its floor boards and Tillie looked at it, sniffed and kicked it off with her foot. She could never take leave of anything, even people and places she had scorned, without a display of emotion, and growled and sulked the better part of that day.

The Quonset hut was every bit as big as the building we had been renting from Mr. Merlin Choate and was better divided too, thanks to Axe Aleywine who knew a thing or two about construction engineering. He, Neppie, and Mr. Leaptrot worked all day erecting room partitions and my father did a willing share too, although at one point in all the frenzy had to confess he didn't know the difference between a two-penny nail and a ten-penny nail. Honey Bunch said that wasn't anything to be ashamed about and Mr. Leaptrot readily agreed. Neppie said in his opinion the church part of the Quonset hut wasn't big enough and my father said well, if his congregation continued to grow he'd just hold services out of doors.

When it was almost evening Hershal and Barton hoisted their pup tent and the boards to form its floor to yet another tree and Tillie squalled that they hadn't provided a ladder so they had to come down and make one, nailing stepping boards to the tree's trunk. Soon it began to grow dark and these three and I sat in the tree house listening to the silence. Birds winged nestward; in neighboring trees they settled down for the night and the lights from the occupied Quonset hut shone yellow through the branches of its own surrounding trees. Presently the early moon cast its light on this strange realm and the four in the tree house began to talk.

"All the birds are asleep," said Tillie.

"Sholey," agreed Hershal. "It's night; they belong to be asleep."

"Mrs. Quisenberry doesn't look like a person who just got out of a hospital," commented Barton. "Know what she told me when she brought the ham and cake for our supper? Said Mr. Merlin Choate takes ugly pills. I wonder could that be true."

"She was just cutting the fool with you," I said. "She loves to joke and have fun. There's no such thing as ugly pills. Don't think about Mr. Merlin Choate any more. We're done with him."

"I don't mind Mrs. Quisenberry," said Hershal. "Or Miss Pearl or Josie Cullers either. They're going to give me a job in their cosmetic company. Mrs. Quisenberry said I could start just as soon as they got all their stuff moved out here."

Tillie was cross because she was tired from the day's hubbub and had lost her hat with the cherries on it. "I don't like it here; there's not enough light. We should have a street light."

"There is the light from the moon," I pointed out. "Look at it. In olden times, before electricity was invented, that's all people had. Listen to the owl. Isn't that the cutest sound? Isn't it nice out here? So quiet and so much peace. It is what everyone wants the most and we have it now. Peace."

Tillie had scooted forward to the door opening of the tree house, was looking out. Reveling in the sinister she said, "Shhhhhh. There's somebody out there. I can feel their voices. They're way up near the creek; on the other side of it. They're coming this way. Listen."

Humoring her, Hershal and Barton pretended to listen. I crawled forward and knelt beside my sister. "I don't hear anything," I said. "Nobody would be out here at night. What for?"

"I don't know," answered Tillie, whispering through her fingers. "Something. I don't know. I feel their voices. They're on this side of the creek now. They aren't walking any more. They've stopped."

Another second of listening. The owl began its hooting again and away in the distance the light from the moon cast its bright reflection on the creek—the moonglade of poets.

"There's nobody out there," I said.

"We shouldn't come out here after dark," said Tillie. "I won't anymore." She was preparing to leave the tree house, urging us to leave with her, hurry, hurry. I was the last to go down the ladder. The others ran ahead of me toward home, blazing their own trail through the trees and grasses, and the voice of the owl followed us.

Sometime during that night a department-store mannequin was placed on the grass in front of our Quonset hut. It was dressed in dark, male clothing, ordinary except for a turned-around collar such as ministers of some denominations wear. Its shiny, painted face was stylishly thin. Its lacquered eyes were fixed in a permanent, wide-open stare. Its red mouth was hidden behind a wide strip of tight, soiled adhesive tape.

Elver thought the dummy was a big fun-doll, a present deposited by some kind, well-meaning person. He wanted to know why it had been left during sleep hours and what was wrong with its mouth. Why was it taped shut? Nobody answered his questions. In the hush of the earliness of the hour, my father and Honey Bunch, both still in their nightclothes, stood looking down at the stiff, flesh-colored figure.

"I would like to think this is just a prank," said Honey Bunch. "But I can't get my mind to go in that direction."

"It's no prank," said my father.

"Then we should call the police," said Honey Bunch.

My father shook his head. "No. No police. No publicity. The best thing to do is ignore it. We'll go inside now and have our breakfast and afterward I'll dispose of this thing." None of us moved. Clustered around the prone mannequin, we stood looking down at its silly, bandaged face and at each other.

Tillie had found her hat. Now again it sat primly atop her head, the dark cherries on its crown wobbling with each emphatic punch of her words. "Woodrow said something like this might happen to us. It's a warning. Some people in this town don't like our church. They want us to leave, I think. I know who it is. It's some men that work for Mr. Merlin Choate. Woodrow told me all about them. He goes to band practice with his father every Wednesday night and hears things. He slips around and listens to his father and the others talk. There are some mean, nasty men Mr. Merlin Choate gets to do stuff like this. He pays them and they do it."

"Hush," said Honey Bunch. "Hush. We're all going to go inside now and have our breakfast and we're going to put this out of our minds."

This was much easier said than done. All during that day there were rumblings and ramblings concerning the mannequin incident. And many plans to get even with the donors of the store-dummy, should they return.

"The next time they come sneaking up here I'm going to be ready for them," declared Tillie. "I'm going to fill up Hershal's water gun with ammonia and put it under my pillow and when I hear them coming I'm going to get out of bed, very quietly, and tiptoe over to the window and let them have it right between the eyes! It'll blind them for life! Won't they be surprised?"

Barton had what he said was a better idea: Buckets of hot tar to be slung in the faces of the low-lifers. Hershal favored a big iron hand (he'd invent it) that would descend from a tree and slap them bowlegged. I tried to think of something that would torment their minds.

"Like what?" asked Tillie with a hopeful gleam.

"I don't know. I am trying to think of something mental that would torment their minds. The trouble is, it isn't *their* minds that did this."

"I am not after anybody's mind," said Tillie. "I like revenge I can see. It might be a sin of the uninstructed, like Daddy says, but nothing makes you feel any better than just to run up and fram the daylights out of somebody who's done something bad to you."

Engaged in a struggle with my imagination, I drew closer to Tillie. "I don't like physical fighting. It makes me sick to my stomach. Remember the time that terrible boy gave Barton a black eye?"

"You like to have killed him," said Tillie and in a rush of loving, sisterly friendship hugged me. "Oh, I'll never forget how you came swinging out of that tree in that old tire! He tried to jump out of the way but you dropped right on top of him and bam, bam! He thought the hound of hell had got him! Oh, how I loved that!"

"I didn't. I hated it. It made me sick to my stomach. I don't like to fight, not even mentally."

"But sometimes you have to," said Tillie.

"Yes."

"Are you going to this time?"

"Maybe. If I can think of something."

"Do you feel anything coming?"

"No."

The Church of Blessed Hope was going to be host for a community sing—an all-day social gathering of the members of the congregation and their friends and relatives and the plans for this, which had been simple at first, were snowballing.

"This bazaar everybody is talking about," I said to Honey Bunch. "Is it going to be in a marketplace with booths?"

Honey Bunch was making vegetable soup and orange biscuits. "No. We'll either have it just outside on the church grounds or choose a site up near the creek. We'll use tables instead of booths."

"When I was at the hospital this morning visiting friends everyone wanted to know about it. Sonny Wages wants me to be one of the merchants. He says I should sell flower chains and dreams."

"Who is Sonny Wages?" asked Honey Bunch.

"He's a man I know. Eighty-two years old. Has to stay in a wheelchair most of the time because he's crippled from arthritis. Crazy about flower chains."

"Flower chains?"

"Every time I go to the hospital I take as many flowers as I can. There's a whole field of them growing wild on Dahlia Street. We make flower chains, Sonny and I. Everybody on his floor comes to his room and we make tea and have a good time. Everybody wants to come to the bazaar, even Dr. Elspeth. He wants to know what day we're going to have it."

"On a Saturday," said Honey Bunch. "The one after next."

"Sonny has got three dollars he's going to spend and Thornia Tucker, that's the lady he's going to marry, has got two. Josie is going to give away samples of her pioneer cosmetics. Sonny and his friends are making them from her recipes. This morning after we got through with the flower chains we made some cucumber cream. I went and got the stuff and everybody worked. Look, I brought you a sample."

Honey Bunch glanced at the little, see-through box that once had contained pills for someone's illness. "Looks nice. Let me smell."

I unscrewed the top of the box and held it to Honey Bunch's nose. "It's for older skins. It's got a tablespoon of honey in it, a teaspoon of rose water, two egg whites, a half teaspoon of milk, and two tablespoons of cucumber juice. And just a little tiny bit of green food coloring. Tomorrow we're going to make some Happy Foot Cream if I can find some marigolds. You're supposed to put marigold petals in it."

"About Sonny Wages," said Honey Bunch. "Did you say he's eighty-two and is about to get married?"

"Yes, and isn't that the most wonderful thing you ever heard? He's never been married before because he's a Taurus and is always slow to decide what he wants to do. He's loved Thornia since he was thirteen years old but had never been able to make up his mind what to do about her. I told him."

"Told him what?" asked Honey Bunch.

"That I thought he'd been messing around long enough. All of his life he's been sending Thornia May baskets and valentines. Taurus people are very careful, all my astrology books say so. I told Sonny that. He asked me to go with him to Thornia's room and let me listen to him propose to her. He was so nervous he forgot to be romantic. All he said was, 'Thornia, we've been messing around long enough now. Will you marry me?' She screamed and said yes. She's eighty."

"Oh, my word," said Honey Bunch.

"Yes. For their honeymoon Mrs. Quisenberry is going to drive them to Lake Sapphire. There's a lodge there and they're going to spend three days and then Mrs. Quisenberry will go back and get them. Thornia isn't allowed to drive a car anymore. She's almost blind."

"Well," said Honey Bunch. "I certainly wish them every happiness."

"Oh, they will be happy," I said. "Happiness is in the stars for them. I helped them plan how they're going to live. Thornia's got a little house and they're going to fix it up and once a week Mrs. Quisenberry will go to the store for them. Sonny loves to cook and iron. He's going to be Thornia's eyes and she's going to be his legs. Josie Cullers is going to give them her washing machine; she and Miss Pearl only need one between them now they're friends—and I'm going to get them a cat. I know where there's one that's going to have kittens pretty soon."

"Delpha," said Honey Bunch, "sometimes you scare me."

"Mama," I said. "You're so funny. I don't scare you. You're just saying that. I don't know how to scare anybody."

VIRGO

THE VIRGIN

AUGUST 24TH THROUGH
SEPTEMBER 23RD

On earth there will be peace
Through Vulcan's release.

NINE

My friend, Sonny Wages, asked me to furnish the flowers for his wedding to Thornia Tucker and I did. Field daisies and black-eyed Susans. I arranged them in buckets and pots borrowed from the hospital kitchen and put them in every corner of Sonny's room. In this I had about a dozen hands to assist. People on Sonny's floor kept popping in and out with suggestions and advice. Somebody hung a sheaf of daisies from the light fixture.

About ten minutes before the ceremony Sonny had the wicked idea to make two chains from some of the blossoms, one to hang around Thornia's neck and one for his own. He wanted to make them himself but was so flustered he was all thumbs so I had to fashion them alone while Sonny wheeled himself furiously around the room, yanked his watch from his pocket ten times, gazed at its face, rolled up to a table stacked with presents, snatched a bar of fancy soap from a box and pressed it to his cheek. He said, "I never knew I had so many friends. Everybody in the hospital. Look at all this soap. Must be ten boxes."

"Twelve," I said. "There was a special on it at the drugstore. Only two kinds though—lemon and lilac. I thought lilac was the nicest and everybody said for me to use my own judgment so that's what I did. Maybe I should have got half and half."

"Oh, no!" cried Sonny. "I love lilac and I'm sure Thornia does too. You have impeccable taste in soap! Absolutely impeccable!" He was so excited he almost forgot about his arthritis. When my father, escorting Thornia, came into the room he nearly fell out of his wheelchair and during the brief ceremony ate one of the daisies from the chain around his neck. When Daddy asked him if he took Thornia to be his lawful, wedded wife, to hold and love until death did them part, he couldn't speak. I had to hop over to him and whisper, "Sonny, you have to tell Daddy whether you take Thornia to be your lawful, wedded wife."

"Oh, yes, I do!" shouted Sonny and then, after the wedding pronouncements had been made, clapped his hands, laughing with all his friends who were crowded into the room. "You promised rice! Where's the rice?" And they pelted him with it and tied strings of tin cans on his wheelchair. Those who were able went down to the porch to watch the newlyweds being driven away by Mrs. Quisenberry.

Mrs. Quisenberry had herself taken a new lease on life. Said her second wind had come up and phooey to anybody that got in the way of it; she'd blow them to heck and gone. Said she knew a good idea from a hole in the ground when she saw one. Women were tired of being flimflammed and lied to and overcharged when they bought cosmetics. What they wanted was simplicity and purity at a reasonable cost and that's what she, Miss Pearl, and Josie Cullers intended to give them and it wasn't anybody's business but theirs, least of all not any of Judge Potter's. Concerning this and also the business of allowing The Church of Blessed Hope to operate from her land and one of her buildings, Judge Potter had been to see her and she had had the pleasure of setting his mind straight on a few things:

Number one, what she did with her money was her own affair and number two, The Church of Blessed Hope was putting some life and sense into the town as anybody with half the brains of a gnat could see. If anybody doubted this all they had to do was walk around some of the neighborhoods to get their eyes opened.

Take the people who lived on Marigold Street for instance, under whom somebody (perhaps more than one body) had kindled a nice little fire that brought them from their houses during every spare second they could scrape, borrow, and beg, to paint and plant and fix up. Due to the brilliance of an old grandmother who, for years, had been disgusted with all the bickering, fighting, and quarreling on this street, disputes were now quickly and efficiently settled.

Her zodiac sign was Virgo, so from birth she had had the gift of inspiring people to their best behavior but only recently had she realized this. Her rule for peacemaking was: "The one who thinks he's right should be the first to shut up and offer to shake hands and say he's sorry."

A new kind of life had come to the people in Chinquapin Cove and now the peace among them deprived Judge Tate Potter of some of his importance. Mrs. Quisenberry said this was slightly unsettling to the judge and said she was glad. Said if the judge didn't like what was happening he could take a flying leap off the nearest rooftop and go into the garden and eat worms too. While he was at it he should feed Merlin Choate a few and shouldn't forget Sheriff Bumper Choate also.

The judge had the nerve to suggest Mrs. Quisenberry was minus some of her marbles and for that received a flower pot in his back as he made his retreat off her porch. The judge, said Mrs. Quisenberry, had better watch out, he had so few marbles of his own left. Merlin Choate wasn't any better, crazier than a bedbug. Wanting to divorce his wife of forty-three years. He had driven her into hiding; she had simply disappeared from the scene. For days nobody had seen her around, not that she was any great loss to the town.

Mrs. Quisenberry told us these things one day while taking lunch with us, and the next came roaring out from town in her Chevrolet station wagon crammed with Miss Pearl, Josie Cullers, Fletcher, cartons containing jars and bottles of all shapes and sizes, an American flag to ripple from a staff atop the Honeysuckle Cosmetic Company, boxes from drug companies containing more jars and bottles of camphor, oil of wintergreen, menthol, lanolin, petroleum jelly, castor oil, oil of lemon, rose oil, glycerine, and mint extract. Fletcher was everywhere underfoot. He was allowed to run loose and kept a stern eye on all the attractive commotion. Tottering around, peering and prying into everything, he cried, "Bless Pat! By jingo! Oh, you're a caution!"

There were a number of immediate problems, the foremost of which was the telephone. It had been installed according to a promise but was deader than a doornail, not even one hum or crackle in its line.

"Those incompetents at the telephone company," said Mrs. Quisenberry. "They promised service not later than today. I suppose I'll have to run back into town and fight with them."

"We've got to have a telephone," said Miss Pearl. "I've got calls to make and calls coming in."

My sister, brothers, and I were present. I said, "If we had a phone you could use it. We don't though. The lady at the telephone company said it might take a year for us to get one."

Mrs. Quisenberry turned to look at me. "A year to get a phone put in? Ridiculous. This isn't a big city. It's Chinquapin Cove."

"Violet," said Miss Pearl to Mrs. Quisenberry, "let's just you and I go back to town and get this matter settled." She picked up Fletcher, kissed the top of his head, and handed him to me. "Stay with Delpha, honey. Mama'll be right back."

"Oh, you're a caution!" said Fletcher and screamed his hideous laugh.

On the way to town Mrs. Quisenberry and Miss Pearl had an accident that laid them both up with contusions and abrasions for over a month. Sheriff Bumper Choate who came out to deliver the news said apparently Mrs. Quisenberry lost control of her automobile as she tried to take a sharp curve in the road. It rolled over once.

Josie lost temporary control of herself. She jumped around five hampers of cucumbers on which she had just accepted delivery a moment before Bumper's arrival, grabbed a handful of Bumper's shirtfront, and there took place a slight scuffle during which Bumper tried to break away but it was as if, somehow, he and Josie had become physically joined. Every time Bumper lifted his feet to move backward Josie lifted hers and moved forward in the same, exact second. If they hadn't been fighting they might have been dancing, so perfectly were their movements equaled. "Josie," panted Bumper. "Now wait a minute, Josie. You got no call to jump on me like this. It's not my fault your friends had an accident. I just brought you the news. I know it's a shock. . . . Now wait a minute, Josie."

"Bumper," said Josie, panting herself. "Why is it all the news you've ever brought me has been bad?"

"Josie, I never brought you any bad news before this!"

"Yes, you did! That time I was going to get married—"

"Josie, that man was a crook. He had bad checks plastered all over this town."

"I told you I didn't care anything about that! He wanted to marry me and I wanted to marry him!"

"Josie, that was ten years ago!"

"You cat killer! Loudmouth! Low-down hot-dogger!"

Bumper was executing some pretty fancy steps; his legs seemed glued to Josie's. He was trying not to touch her with his hands. His countrified face was red as a beet. "Josie, you better watch out who you're callin' a loudmouth and cat killer and low-down hot-dogger. It ain't no sin for me to like hot dogs. You better watch out, callin' me those names. I'm sheriff of this county and I don't stand for no public profanity!"

Josie said later she had known for years that Bumper was supremely ignorant but when he accused her of using public profanity when all she had called him was a cat killer and low-down hot-dogger and loudmouth she was so surprised she let go of him and he ran from the building, jumped in his car, and drove off.

To catch her breath Josie sat down on one of the hampers of cucumbers. One of her stockings had come loose from its hidden fastening and slipped down in a twist around her leg. She rested her eyes on those of us who had watched the ruckus in solemn silence. "Well," she said. "It could have been worse I suppose. Yes, of course it could. Bumper said just some contusions and abrasions. I guess the first thing I'd better do is get your father to drive me to the hospital. Would one of you go tell him what's happened and ask him please?"

"We can't right now," I said. "He's gone with Mama

to buy Elver new shoes. He'll be back in a little bit, then he'll take you, I am sure. You kind of look queer, Josie. You feel all right?"

"Oh, yes," replied Josie almost gaily. "I need a minute to collect myself. . . . My business partners . . . My friends—" A stark thought widened her eyes. "We'll lose. Pearl has already spent a small fortune in advertising. What will I do? I can't handle it all. We were supposed to start manufacturing today."

"Maybe," said Tillie who enjoyed an emergency, "we could help you manufacture."

"We were going to start with the cucumber cream," said Josie, weak and lonely. "And the containers—there's only one sample finished. They have to be painted with our trademark. That was Pearl's department."

"Mama can paint," said Hershal. "So can Barton. What's your trademark?"

"A honeysuckle sprig," said Josie and in that exact moment the telephone rang.

"Somebody at the telephone company woke up and fixed it," said Barton. "Isn't that funny?"

Fletcher shrieked, "Bless Pat! By jingo!" And all Josie did was look at the phone. I had to take it up and speak to Woodrow's father at the post office who said he had a relative who collected odd postmarks. He had put several letters in the box for the Honeysuckle Cosmetic Company from some odd-sounding places—Sopchoppy and Ditty Wa Ditty and Kopesetic. Would it be all right, he asked, if he just snipped the postmarks from the envelopes?

"Sir," I said. "I cannot say. Miss Pearl and Mrs.

Quisenberry just had a car accident. They are both in the hospital with abrasions and contusions and Josie Cullers is sitting here on some cucumbers, weak and about to pass out from shock. Should I ask her to phone you back as soon as she gets feeling a little better?"

"I'd be obliged," said Woodrow's father. "Do I know you?"

"Probably through your little son Woodrow you do, sir. I am Delpha Green."

"Oh, yes," said Woodrow's father. "The Water Bearer."

"Yes, sir. Some people call me that."

"Woodrow is very fond of you and your sister and brothers," said Woodrow's father.

"Yes, sir. We are fond of Woodrow too. He is a smart little tyke and, if I may say so, charming company also."

"He has a terrific imagination. He thinks a mugwump lives in the woods back of our house. He had me out there with him this morning hardly before the sun was up trying to get a look at it."

"Mugwumps are such cute birds. The way they sit around on stumps with their mugs on one end and their wumps on the other."

Woodrow's father chuckled. "He wants to get close enough to one to put salt on its tail."

"Well," I said. "He might not ever get to do that. Only two people in the whole world have ever seen a mugwump."

"You and who else?" asked Woodrow's father, all abrim with curiosity.

"There was a fellow up in Kentucky who one time got a look at one," I said. "He was a man something like Daniel Boone. Woodrow knows about him; I told him. Watching for mugwumps is a lot better occupation than pounding nails all day long, don't you think?"

"Oh, the nails Woodrow used to pound!" exclaimed Woodrow's father. "Before he got this interest in mugwumps he used to drive both his mother and me nearly crazy pounding nails. Never made anything, you understand. Just pounded nails from morning to night. Spent all his allowance and then some on nails. I bet he put twenty pounds of them in our front porch."

"He is certainly an energetic child," I commented.

"I am in your debt," said Woodrow's father who was a little on the old-fashioned side, "for taking an interest in Woodrow."

"I will tell Josie about the postmarks and she will call you back pretty soon," I said.

Josie said Woodrow's father was welcome to any and all postmarks on letters addressed to the Honeysuckle Cosmetic Company. All she was interested in was the orders inside the envelopes which were pitiful to say the least, not at all measuring up to expectations. Josie said she didn't have the heart to show them to Mrs. Quisenberry and Pearl. They were in no condition to receive any discouraging news. They were doped to the eyebrows, Josie said, on pain killers but even so they were suffering, each with feet of missing skin, swellings the size of oranges, and navy-blue bruises. Mrs. Quisenberry's son and his wife were scared silly they would be asked to take Mrs. Quisenberry into their home and care for her until she was on her feet again.

"That pair," said Josie. "They got me out in the hall and you never heard such gripey whining in all your days."

"Josie," said Honey Bunch. "Please eat your soup."

"It's all Merlin Choate's fault," said Josie, working up some wrathful indignation. "The roads around here are .nothing but death traps. They should have been widened and straightened years ago but Merlin doesn't want that. He's afraid if we had decent roads people would come from the outside and spoil what he's got here so he's used his in fluence. I don't understand a person like Merlin. I think he must have ice water in his veins instead of blood." She leaned her head into her hands and her tears fell into her soup. "I wish I had ice water in *my* veins instead of blood. Then I wouldn't feel anything. Like Merlin. And I'd be happy. Other people's troubles wouldn't bother me. Life is hurtful, mine has always been. Violet's and Pearl's too. I know about their lives. Violet laughs when she talks about her son and his wife but she's been hurt by them. By every-thing. The same as you, Reverend Green. And you, Honey Bunch. Your children too."

"No," said Honey Bunch. "No, Josie."

"Yes," whispered Josie and her tears rained into her soup. She pressed her fingers over her eyes, seeming to try to stop the tears which wouldn't stop and her voice came, frail as an autumn leaf, timid and apologizing for what she spoke. She was our friend and meant no harm; there was only hurt truth in what she said. "Yes. Oh, yes. Don't tell me. I know. Everybody knows what you were before you got to be what you are now and all of you had to have been hurt by it. Life hurts people. Sometimes I think that's all it's for. If we could all be like Merlin Choate and hold ourselves away from things and people the way he does . . . If we could do that, we'd be better off."

The noonday sun had spangled the windows with its light. It fell across the figure of my father in his chair at the head of the table. I saw his eyes kindle. He directed what he said to Josie but he was speaking to all of us. He had the face of a gifted person and all of us, Honey Bunch, Josie, Tillie, Barton, Hershal, and I, saw him then as the members of his growing congregation must always have seen him—as a gifted teacher. He said to us, "I wouldn't be better off. I would be suffocated by this life if I didn't allow myself to feel everything God gave me the nature to feel. I want to experience it all and want this for my wife and children too. Even the parts of our lives that hurt us and inspire us with despair and make us afraid. God did not prohibit these emotions. They are the deepest feelings we have in our natures. They are all a part of this great adventure we call life and I would not hide myself from them merely to keep myself safe."

Josie was not ready to give up. In a lingering, lonesome voice she said, "Reverend, you make me feel like a sinner. Not to want to experience the bad things along with the good. Of course I have heard you say things like this before; they have brought the people to you. But it never really dawned on me till just now . . . Well, isn't it funny how you can hear things but not hear them at the same time? Until just now I never thought about the bad things that happen to me or my friends as being any kind of a worthwhile experience. I always thought just to try and be cheerful when the bad things came."

My father was not looking at me but his next words were as if they were for me alone. It was like reading a poem and surprising upon a phrase that was concerned with my secret self, the one that always had to look for the rainbow and find it and thrust it on other people. I heard him speak and all that I had involved myself in on his behalf grew small. Foolish even. He said, "Well, cheerfulness can be a friend during bad times but to meet every bitter occurrence with a smile and an excuse is not a true human quality."

There. A little powerful chill of something running down my spine. A falling away of the feelings that had so long been a part of me they were habits. Ah, to let the tears fall over bitter occurrences and let fear and anxiousness be felt and do away with the smile I had thought meant so much. To do away with the always-cheerfulness that had been awful at times. Yes, it had been. When it wasn't real it was awful. Not to do away with the astrology though. The astrology was a little like church-religion, grand and enlarging. To think that the stars and the moon and planets might make one person this way and another person that way was like thinking of the power of God. And who could think about either without feeling his own smallness?

My father's words made their claim on me. Early in the afternoon Honey Bunch sent Tillie, Barton, Hershal, and me to the woods to gather honeysuckle sprigs. These were to be models for Honey Bunch when she decorated the jars that would contain the cosmetics manufactured by the Honeysuckle Cosmetic Company. To find the plants we had to cross the creek by jumping from rock to rock and on the other side of it we went up to higher ground. The goldenrod was in bloom. Under a thorny toothache tree we came upon a dead squirrel. It had only been gone a minute or so, for it was still soft and warm.

To me Hershal said, "It was old, I think."

"Yes. But I wish we could have got here sooner so that it needn't have died alone."

"Animals don't mind dying alone. They aren't afraid to die."

"Oh, how do you know?"

"That's what you said when our dog died. And you wouldn't let any of us feel bad."

"I was wrong to do that. I should have let you feel what you wanted to feel."

"Delpha," said Tillie, most gravely. "Everything's got to go sometime or another."

"Yes. Can we dig a little grave, do you think?"

They didn't laugh at me for wanting that. After the burial we laid spikes of goldenrod on the grave.

Late in the afternoon of this day, I and my troupe, returning from our expedition in the woods, passed beneath the tree house in the woods closer to home and heard a sound that wasn't either bird or animal. We stood rock-still, looking at each other puzzled. We listened to the sound coming from the pup tent, a rough female voice talking to itself, breaking off every few words to laugh. This wasn't the laugh of anyone gone mad. It was the sound of one who is pleased, who is enjoying a secret joke. There was a little rustle and a box that had contained soda crackers came sailing out of the doorway of the pup tent. It fell through the foliage of the tree to the ground. This was followed by a drumstick that had been picked clean of all its meat.

We made signs to each other. We went up the board ladder into the tree. Sure enough the pup tent was occupied. Mrs. Merlin Choate had taken up residence in it.

PISCES

THE FISH

FEBRUARY 20TH THROUGH MARCH 20TH

Floating downstream in life's
Whirl of Neptunian rosiness.

TEN

It was such a peculiar thing for her to be there. She wasn't much to look at. Dumpy was the word for her, with such dreary hair and her clothes looked as if they had been snatched from the rag bag. She wore a lot of vulgar jewelry. Seated on a suitcase she was eating yellow cheese. She spoke to us peering, interested Greens calmly, as if every day she roosted in a strange tree house, receiving callers. "Hey," she said. "Come on in."

Mrs. Merlin Choate acted as if it was not all a novel situation. She took the hem of her dress to her mouth and wiped away the bits of stray, clinging cheese. Her possum eyes were bland as butter. She was very much out of tune with any ladylike qualities.

With a creaking of the floor boards, Hershal, Tillie, and Barton were arranging themselves against the canvas walls. They were agog with interest but politely withheld their curiosity. With a great show of nonchalance Tillie rubbed the pink button on her hat and Barton blackened his front teeth with Black Jack gum. Hunkered on her suitcase, Mrs. Choate slid her eyes from face to face. Her expression said: This is a commonplace situation and don't try to make it anything else. She asked a question: "Don't I know you all? Ain't you renting one of my houses?"

"We were," I replied. "But Judge Potter made us move. We live out here now."

Mrs. Choate received this information with a quick blinking of her eyes, nothing else. She was concerned with what was left of the cheese, wrapping it in a piece of brown, oiled paper. The silver bracelets on her arms clinked against each other. "How far you live from here?"

"Not far," I said.

"Is this your tree house?"

"It belongs to my sister and brothers. They built it."

"You did a good job hiding it," said Mrs. Choate, complaining this fact peevishly. "I must have gone by it half a dozen times before I happened to look up. I was lookin' for a place to hide. Like to have broke my fool neck gettin' up here with this suitcase. It's heavy."

"Speaking for my sister and brothers," I said, "you are welcome to the hospitality of this little house. How long are you planning on staying?"

Mrs. Choate was rummaging through her purse. She found lipstick and without the aid of a mirror applied a generous smear to her mouth. The pure, hard red of its color was all wrong for the sallow tone of her skin. Her elbows, I noted, were very dirty. She looked quite a bit like her husband. Probably nothing ever fazed her. In response to my question she said, "I don't know how long I'm planning on stayin' up here. Maybe just another minute. Your daddy's a preacher, ain't he?"

"He's a minister," I answered.

Mrs. Choate was amused. "A minister and a preacher is the same thing, honey. Don't be so touchy. Is there anybody at your home besides you kids and your mama and daddy?"

"No," I said, forgetting Josie Cullers.

"If you was to take me home with you, you reckon your mama would sell me a cup of coffee? I'm dyin' for one."

"No," said Tillie, coming to life. "She won't sell you one but she'll give you one." And quick as a dart of lightning Mrs. Merlin Choate got to her feet. Hershal offered to carry her suitcase for her but she said, "No, I'll do it. You should go ahead of me and make sure I don't fall gettin' out of this tree. You watch me and make sure I don't slip, hear?"

We took Mrs. Merlin Choate out of the tree house and out of the woods. She walked the distance to our house briskly, loitering once or twice in the pathways to rest her suitcase and spit into the sparkleberry bushes. She was as crude as her husband and I could not think one good thought of her. Observing her, a wicked thought went scrambling through my mind: Mr. Merlin Choate and this woman should not be allowed a divorce. They are alike and should have to live together for the rest of their days.

Honey Bunch and my father were polite about having Mrs. Merlin Choate for our guest. My father offered the best chair and Honey Bunch put fresh coffee on to perk and then Josie came out of a back room. She looked at Mrs. Choate and started not to speak but Honey Bunch said, "Josie, we have a guest."

"I see we have," said Josie, nodding to Mrs. Choate. "How are you, Hattie Mae?"

"I'll do," answered Mrs. Choate. That she disliked Josie showed in her slitted eyes and the downward pull of her mouth.

"Pearl Drawhorne and Violet Quisenberry had a bad automobile accident this morning, Hattie Mae," said Josie.

"Is that right?" said Mrs. Choate. "I hadn't heard. You look some different since the last time I seen you, Josie. You've let your hair grow out to its natural color, haven't you?"

"Yes," answered Josie, grinning, and let a couple of seconds go by before asking, "How's that old goat, skinflint husband of yours, Hattie Mae? Did anybody take a potshot at him yet in a dark alley? Don't worry, they'll get around to it sure as my name is Josie Cullers. I swear, Hattie Mae, you sure don't get any better-looking, do you? It's no wonder to me Merlin wants to divorce you, which is not to say I think he's any prize catch either."

Mrs. Merlin Choate wasn't about to take this criticism of her husband lying down. If looks could have killed, Josie would have dropped dead on the spot. Said Mrs. Choate, "You must be blind, Josie. Merlin's the best-looking man in this town when he's dressed up, ask anybody."

"If you like 'em scarecrow," said Josie. "Merlin's so skinny he could swim in a garden hose. He ought to try eating a square meal sometime. It'd cost him a little bit more than just tea and toast three times a day but he can afford it. He can't take his money with him when he dies. Neither can you, Hattie Mae."

Mrs. Choate jerked around, snaked her foot out and placed it *clump* on top of her suitcase which was on the floor beside her chair and Josie cried, "Aha! I might have known it! That suitcase is full of money! For crying out loud, Hattie Mae! You get more like Merlin every day. I don't know what he wants to divorce you for. He'd never find another one like you. He wouldn't know what to do with a normal woman."

There might have been a fight between Josie and Mrs. Choate had not Honey Bunch jumped in between them. She said, "Josie, that kind of talk is not nice. This lady is our guest."

"Sorry," said Josie, not sorry one bit.

Mrs. Choate drank her coffee and from then on ignored Josie; directed all of her conversation to Honey Bunch and my father: "I guess you've heard about the little trouble my husband and me are havin'. I'm not running away from it, you understand. I just need a little time to get things sorted out in my mind. Merlin don't really want to put me in the crazy house. He's just a little mixed up hisself. I feel like if I could just lay down and sleep a while . . . Could you let me stay here tonight?"

"Oh," said Honey Bunch quickly, "I'm sorry. We don't have any extra rooms. Not even one."

"I could sleep with one of the kids," said Mrs. Choate and sniffed her grubby tears. "It's awful not to have a place to go. I need to lay down and rest. I need time to think. I spent last night at the Kum-Back Motel. Their beds are harder'n brickbats. I'd pay you if you'd let me stay here tonight."

"No," said my father. "We couldn't take any money from you." Neither he nor Honey Bunch ever did grant Mrs. Choate permission to stay but she stayed.

That night Tillie slept on a pallet beside the bed she and I usually occupied and I tried sleeping in the bed with Mrs. Choate but the conditions were unsuitable. In fact they were almost desperate. Around three o'clock in the morning I decided I could no longer stand them, wrested my pillow from Mrs. Choate and went to Tillie's pallet. She and I lay awake until dawn, whispering.

"I don't like to breathe the same air as her," said Tillie.

"Shhhhhh. She'll hear us."

"No, she won't. She's dead to the world. Old cow."

"She hit me in the eye with one of her dirty elbows."

"Can you think of anything good to say about her?"

"Not one thing."

"Want me to go get some ice to put on your eye?"

"No. I just want to stay here with you. This pallet

smells so nice. She almost suffocated me up there in the bed."

"Here, Sister, let me cover you. There now. Isn't that nice?"

"Nice," I whispered. Across the room in the bed Mrs. Merlin Choate was snoring. *Caaaaaaaa. Ffffffffff, caaaaaaaa.* We two on the pallet shivered our distaste for the vulgar guest and drew closer to each other, continuing our whisperings.

Said Tillie, "She's got a paper she's been trying to get twenty-five people to sign. It says she's a sane, sensible woman and a fine, upstanding member of this community with the interests of the people at heart. It says she's been a good and loving wife to Mr. Merlin Choate. She showed it to Josie and me. Josie laughed at it. Nobody has signed it so far."

"She's an astrological mistake," I said. "According to my books she should be sorry for mankind and be kind and helpful. Instead she's only sorry for herself and she's rude and selfish. She didn't even ask why Judge Potter made us get out of the house she rented us. Didn't ask about how bad Miss Pearl and Mrs. Quisenberry were hurt either. She's not a Fish at all."

"A Fish, Sister?"

"According to her sun sign she's Pisces, the Fish. My books are wrong about her. It makes me feel bad. It's the first mistake I've caught them in."

Still in a ghostly whisper, Tillie said, "Maybe she's mixed up about when she was born. Josie Cullers wouldn't sign her paper but she said wouldn't it be funny if everybody in town would. Then Mr. Merlin Choate couldn't say she was crazy anymore. He'd have to take her back to live with him."

I put my arms across my face. The undesirable one on the bed on the opposite side of the room had turned up her snoring volume. *CAAAAAAAAAA, FFFFFFFFFFT, CAAAAAAAAAA,* and a bird on some mysterious night mission flew over our Quonset hut. My sister and I heard the almost indistinct whirring of its wings as it passed over our roof.

Things got very circumstantial then to say the least. For several days Mrs. Merlin Choate continued to be our guest though she certainly was not wanted. As if it were her right to decide whether to go or stay, several times each day she'd mention leaving and hopes would rise but then she'd design to look sick and lonely and say, "No, I can't go today. Tomorrow maybe. If I'm being any trouble to you I'll pay you for whatever you think it's worth. Just let me stay another day." Of course we couldn't, wouldn't take any money from her.

Finally to relieve the situation Josie took the unwelcome guest across the way to the Honeysuckle Cosmetic Company and tried to interest her in some of her pioneer recipes: Josie's Cure for Red Noses, Josie's Gay-Fling Foot Cream, Josie's Sheen-Skin (this lent instant, pearly beauty to dull complexions), and so on.

After a curious, knowledgeable look around Mrs.

Choate gave a vinegar opinion: "Well, you might make out. I doubt it though. It's pretty country and old-fashioned. Women nowadays buy their cosmetics in drugstores. Personally, I think it's crazy."

Huddled like a graduate witch over a pot of steaming brew, Josie said, "Do you? I don't. It might be unusual but it's not crazy. The word crazy is the most misused and overworked one in our whole language. People use it when they don't understand things and people. It's like credible. Anything's credible when you look at it right. If I told you I was in love with a mule one time would you believe it, Hattie Mae? Would you think that was credible?"

"No," answered Mrs. Merlin Choate. "That wouldn't be credible. That'd be crazy."

"Well," said Josie, bending to her pot, "you see, it's all in the choice of words. I say for me to be in love with a mule is credible. You say it's crazy. I can't say I'm right and you can't say you're right because neither of us knows. What we might need is some more opinions. Let's ask our young friends here." The steam from Josie's pot had risen to envelop her head. Through its white, damp mist she smiled at us younger Greens, myself, Tillie, Hershal, and Barton— all of whom were now, in a manner of speaking, employed by the Honeysuckle Cosmetic Company. We were busy at various tasks; Hershal was measuring alum which was one of the ingredients for the Red Nose Cure, Tillie was chopping lemons, Barton was shredding marigold blossoms, I was spooning Josie's Sheen-Skin into little jars. Josie's face, covered with the glistening steam-mist, seemed to spring at me. Josie said, "Delpha, you're a smart little girl. If I told you I was in love with a mule would you say that's credible or would you say it's crazy?"

"It's credible," I said, and through my lashes watched Mrs. Choate.

Josie said, "Tillie?"

"Credible," said Tillie. "If you want to be in love with a mule you've got a right."

"Credible," said Barton.

"If you wanted to be in love with a mule that would be your business," said Hershal. "It's not crazy. It is sholey credible."

Josie turned her relaxed smile on Mrs. Merlin Choate. "You see? What's crazy and what is not is all in the minds of the beholders. Like I said before, Hattie Mae, crazy is a misused and overworked word and people should be more careful how they apply it."

Mrs. Merlin Choate pushed her hand up and down her arm, clanking her bracelets. "Mules are cussed and ornery. The only way to get along with one is to let him know who's boss and you got to do this right off too, otherwise you'll wind up doing all the heavy work while he does the light. Merlin and I had one, one time. Wasn't worth a plugged nickel. He chewed his rope loose one day and ran away from us. We never did find out where he went to; he never came back."

"He must have been intelligent," suggested Josie.

"Merlin's a good man," flashed Mrs. Choate. "He never mistreated that mule. Just chastised him a little whenever he did wrong. Merlin's a just man."

Josie lifted her head and gazed for the longest time, first at Mrs. Choate and then at each of us Greens. The steam rising to her face from her simmering pot made her face look delicate. Tenderly, as if in sympathy, she said this to Mrs. Choate: "Hattie Mae, I loved a mule one time and I don't ask you to understand it. You love Merlin and that's the same thing. Nobody but you needs to understand it. You two belong together and should spend the rest of your lives together. Now I know Merlin is saying you're crazy and he's trying to send you off to the crazy house. You've got to stop him. He doesn't know what he's doing. I know men like the palm of my hand. They go through some pretty giddy stages. Merlin's going through one right now and you can bet your bottom dollar on it. He's right on the verge of making a disastrous mistake, trying to put you away. He'll wake up later on but by that time it'll be too late. It's not so easy getting somebody out of a crazy house, once they've been put there. Hattie Mae, you've got to stop Merlin from making this disastrous mistake. You've got to stop him. Hattie Mae?"

"What?" said Hattie Mae Choate, leaning forward.

"Hattie Mae," said Josie. "I've changed my mind about signing that paper of yours. I want to sign it. I want to see justice done. Go get the paper."

Like a shot Mrs. Merlin Choate was off the box on which she had been ungracefully sitting. She went loping to the door but when she reached it she turned back to fretfully say, "But I need twenty-five to sign. You're just one."

"Hattie Mae," said Josie, "just go get the paper. Justice is going to triumph this time, sure enough. My little friends here have all got nice, strong, young legs. I will appoint them as your messengers and mine. They will go out into the town and get you twenty-five signatures. They will get you a hundred signatures. You shouldn't say anything to anybody about this though. Don't even tell Reverend Green or Mrs. Green. Just go get the paper, Hattie Mae, and you lie low like you have been. A little patience will be needed."

"I'll get my paper," said Mrs. Choate and went jumping out the door so fast she almost fell. After she was out of sight and earshot, Josie said to nobody in particular, "Well, I *was* in love with a mule once. He belonged to my granddaddy and I was seven years old. Isn't it funny what keen memories us Sagittarius people have? Generous natures too. I don't 'specially like Hattie Mae Choate but here I am about to do her a kindness. You know, I always read my horoscope in the paper each morning while I'm drinking my coffee. This morning it said I was going to be a big influence in somebody's life today. A Pisces person, it said. And Hattie Mae Choate is a Pisces person. Isn't that the strangest thing?"

"My books made a mistake about her," I said.

"Honey," said Josie, stirring her brew, "that don't matter. It's a lesson, kind of. To teach you books can make mistakes too. After all, people write them, don't they?"

ARIES

THE RAM

MARCH 21ST THROUGH APRIL 20TH

*Today's egocentric infant
Dwelling in the horns of Mars.*

ELEVEN

One day in the early morning of another day, my sister, brothers, and I met some of our friends on the lawn in front of Woodrow Carpenter's house. Among these and closest to my thirteen years was Purple Bubble Gum who wore a black eye-patch. I asked her what for and she said, "Don't be funny. It's my last year to be a child. Yours too. Isn't this fun? Where's Mrs. Choate's petition? That's what my father calls it. A petition. Oh, this looks nice and official. An eye for an eye and a tooth for a tooth. That's what we're gonna give Mr. Merlin Choate. And tit for tat. Right?"

"Right."

With a lamblike expression, Purple Bubble Gum said, "My aunt went back to Biloxi."

"That is good news," I said.

"You bet," said Purple Bubble Gum, jumping around like a monkey. "The day after you were over to my house last time she called up the bank that fired her for being so crabby and told them she had found out why. Told them she had found out the reason she snapped and barked at people was due to her sun sign. They said what sun sign and she told them about being Aries, the Ram. They said, okay, you can have your job back. My mother said they must be desperate. My aunt can do the work of five people while they're just standing around thinking about it. But anyway, she packed up her things and left. My dad said for us to come to his office and he'll sign Mrs. Choate's petition. He's going to get everybody in his office to sign too. It won't take any coaxing." A shiny bubble of blown purple bubble gum slowly came out of the mouth of my friend, lingered delicately and collapsed against her face. She picked it off and popped it back into her mouth. "My dad wants me to be like you. He says you and your father have changed the complexion of this whole town."

"I have changed in the last day or two," I said. "You will find this out. From now on I am going to show everything I feel. I am not going to pretend like I see a rainbow when I don't."

"Well," said Purple Bubble Gum. "That is all right with me."

We were waiting for Woodrow who was inside his house rushing around, searching for his seven-league boots while, at the same time, engaging in a fierce conversation with his mother. "But I tol' you where I was going ten times! I'm going mugwump hunting with the others and they can't wait all day! Where are my boots? What'd you do with them? Oh, here they are. Help me put them on. Where's my box of mugwump salt? You didn't throw it out, did ya?"

"You have to eat!" cried Woodrow's mother. Her voice came to us through the open doors and windows. "You're not going to step one inch out of this house until you do!"

Woodrow came rushing to the front door. Forgetting the earliness of the hour he screamed, "I hafta eat! It won't take me but a minute! Don't leave without me!"

Purple Bubble Gum said, "Isn't Woodrow sweet? His parents are too. I still think we should ask them to be among the first to sign our petition. I am sure they would be glad to. They are people who believe in doing what is right. Remember how they helped me and my family stick up for you and your family when you first came here and some people were calling your father a jailbird?"

"You had better not remind me of that again," I said. "I told you I was through looking for rainbows."

Soon Woodrow came charging from his house and down the steps as fast as his chubby legs would carry him. In the way that children do when the summer has wearied and there are still days of it left and they are bored, he was letting his fondness for excitement and play-theatrics run away with him. Clutching his box of mugwump salt, he leaped through the crowd to me. His passion was causing him to pant. "You got the paper? Well, come on, let's go before my mother thinks of something else for me to do! Out the gate! Everybody! Hurry!"

"Woodrow," I said, running beside him. "Don't run. Wait."

"What for?" cried Woodrow and recklessly threw his box of mugwump salt into the brush. "We should start with that first house down there. The white one. My cousin lives in it. Four other cousins too. They'll all sign. They hate Mr. Merlin Choate. Gimme the paper."

"Woodrow, you shouldn't get so excited—"

"Gimme the paper! You and the rest wait for me over there under that tree! I'll only be a second!" Woodrow bounded off down the street. There was a low stone wall around the white house. Woodrow went over it as if pursued by one of his fictional fiends. He streaked across the grass and went zipping up the steps of the house. In five minutes he was back. "Everybody signed, just like I told you they would. Okay, let's go! Everybody on their feet! Hut, two, three, four!"

"One of his uncles is a drill sergeant in the Marines," Purple Bubble Gum said to me, explaining Woodrow's military language. "Isn't he sweet?"

Hut, two, three, four. Our little company moved down the street and the sun rose higher. The gray crows from the nearby hills flew over the town.

Hut, two, three, four. Woodrow's energy was bottomless and it seemed that both he and Purple Bubble Gum had more relatives than any two people should be decently allowed. Purple Bubble Gum's grandmother, who operated a

134

roominghouse, not only signed Mrs. Merlin Choate's petition herself but got eight of her roomers to sign it. And not only that, she invited my company and me to her kitchen for refreshment.

Hut, two, three, four. Woodrow would not let anybody slow down. Coming out of the office building where Purple Bubble Gum's father worked I said, "Listen, Woodrow. We've got seventy-five signatures and that's enough. Let's quit now."

"Are you crazy?" he screamed. "We've got to give everybody their chance! They're all expecting us because everybody's been telephoning ahead! Come on, let's go!"

Storekeepers and hospital patients, barbers, a street sweeper, three old, bent ladies wheeling groceries home in a baby carriage. Everybody wanted to sign the petition. "Of course Mrs. Merlin Choate is not crazy," they said. "She's just a little eccentric. We have never seen her do one single thing that was not sane and sensible. She's a good and loving wife to Merlin and a fine, upstanding member of our community. Let me borrow one of your ballpoint pens, dear. I don't seem to have one." Behind their eyelids they knew things. They smiled at all of us and to me they said, "We're coming to your community sing and bazaar. Sonny Wages said you were going to sell dreams. Are you really?"

LIBRA

THE SCALES

SEPTEMBER 24TH THROUGH
OCTOBER 23RD

Pretty is as pretty does,
Even with the dimples of Venus.

TWELVE

I should not report that when Mrs. Merlin Choate went back to living with Mr. Merlin Choate she made a good, kind, and loving man of him for that was not the case at all.

A woman who lived close to the Choates told Mrs. Quisenberry that Mr. Choate had taken up the queer habit of wearing earmuffs around the house and spent an awful lot of time in his garage. "I see a light on over there sometimes burning all night long," she said. "I thought he might be making a bomb or something like that so one night I sneaked over for a look. He was sitting in his car, just sitting there staring at nothing. I pecked on one of the windows and said *Boo* and he liked to have jumped out of his skin. He told me his nerves were killing him and I don't wonder. Hattie Mae never lets up on him. I swear that woman has got a voice on her like a foghorn. If it bothered me I'd have to move but fortunately I've got the kind of mind that can close itself to other people's troubles."

At one time the people of Chinquapin Cove had been intensely interested in the personal lives of Mr. and Mrs. Choate but now they were so concerned with their own situations and circumstances they only had time to be vaguely amused at what reportedly went on in the big Choate house.

In the middle of the stream, so to speak, Axe Aleywine decided against his statue of Theodore Roosevelt. He erased what had already been accomplished, had Mr. Leaptrot haul his block of stone down to the town square, and began work on two smaller figures that eventually would be cupids. Some civic-minded ladies said that cupids should be set in the middle of a splashing fountain and one of them marched across to Judge Potter's office and said, "See here, Judge, the looks of this town are a crying shame and we're tired of it. We're going to fix it up and we need some money. Just open up that little tin box of yours and give us some." The judge whined and stalled, as if the money was his and not the taxpayers', and the woman got tired of listening to him and reached over and removed the box from the judge's desk drawer. The judge hollered that he'd have her put in jail and the woman said, "Don't be silly. Sheriff Bumper Choate's too tired to put anybody in jail. His mama makes him so nervous he's moved to the Kum-Back Motel and he hasn't had a decent night's sleep for a week. Nobody but a corpse could sleep in their beds, they're so hard."

Not on the Saturday it had been originally planned but on another, later one The Church of Blessed Hope held its community sing and bazaar. It was a day-long affair and quite a fine, rambunctious time was had by all. Lots of songs were sung and there was much good-natured bartering at the tables which offered such things for sale as candles, homemade fireplace brooms and berry baskets, flower chains, dreams, tea aprons, divinity fudge, Sleeping Beauty Dew Kreme (for refining the texture of the skin while sleeping), hot, buttered roasting ears and cornshuck door mats. There was a pie-eating contest and Sonny Wages won it, but refused his prize which was a big butterscotch confection with a four-inch meringue. He said he never again wanted to see another pie.

There were only a couple of minor fights, the most important of these being between Purple Bubble Gum and Woodrow. Purple Bubble Gum wanted to compete with the boys in the greased pole contest and Woodrow declared this to be a contest strictly for boys. Purple Bubble Gum said, "Is that so? I will tell you something maybe you don't know, Woodrow Carpenter. Nothing in this world is strictly for boys. Women have been liberated and we can do anything we want to now. We're stronger than you so you better not push us anymore." Said Woodrow, "You better get away from that pole if you don't want a fat tomato in your face. This is strictly a contest for boys." Purple Bubble Gum did a shocking thing then. She jerked her skirt up, tucking it in around the waist elastic on her pants, and went up the pole. Clear to the top which was something none of the boys, thus far, had been able to do. Her pants covered her as decently as any pair of walking shorts would have, still it wasn't a nice thing to do. Her mother ordered her to come down and when she did Woodrow let her have a big, fat tomato in her face. She was much larger than Woodrow and got him down on the ground and probably would have murdered him had it not been for her mother's intervention. Her mother snatched Purple Bubble Gum to her feet and shook her hard. "The very idea," she said. "Just look at you. You should be ashamed of yourself."

Purple Bubble Gum wasn't a bit ashamed of herself. As soon as her mother went back to her own activities, she pranced over to where Autumn Lea Nation and I were taking a little rest in a spot of shade, plumped herself down between us, and blew the biggest gum bubble ever. It was beautiful and lasted several minutes before collapsing against her face like a purple spider. Autumn Lea looked at this mess in disgust and coldly said, "You are a revolting child."

"You are mistaken," said Purple Bubble Gum. "I might be revolting but I am not a child. Woodrow just asked me to marry him. Now if I was a child do you think he'd do that?"

"Absolutely revolting," said Autumn Lea. "Delpha is wrong about you. If you have a noble soul and always seek the higher pathways you are not showing it now."

Purple Bubble Gum yawned. "Autumn Lea, I think you are jealous."

"Of what?" demanded Autumn Lea.

"Of my noble soul. I can't help it if I've got one. It's the fault of my zodiac sign which is Capricorn."

"I am a Libra," said Autumn Lea, aloof and haughty. "And have plenty of nobleness in my own soul without being jealous of yours. We Libras have it all over you Capricorns. We don't have to be always showing off to prove ourselves. Especially in public."

"Well," said Purple Bubble Gum, "maybe that's true. But where I've got you beat is, I could sit in a corner by myself for the rest of my life and be happy but you couldn't. You've always got to have people around you."

Autumn Lea could not argue this point. In a minute or so the conversation turned from personalities to other, broader things.

The day was coming to a close and to celebrate the coming of evening my two friends and I took a little stroll into town. We saw Mr. Merlin Choate sitting alone in his car on a dim side street. We were talking and he must have heard our voices but he did not turn his head to look at us.

"Why do you think he's sitting there like that?" asked Purple Bubble Gum.

"He is probably hiding from his wife," said Autumn Lea.

"He is so ugly and lonesome-looking," said Purple Bubble Gum.

ABOUT THE AUTHORS

Vera and Bill Cleaver, whose insights into the wisdom and dignity of young people have proclaimed them among the best-loved writers of contemporary children's books, have been twice nominated for the distinguished National Book Award. They began their career in writing for young people with their unforgettable portrait of *Ellen Grae*, and continue to produce equally compelling stories and characters which have played a part in changing the course of children's literature today.

Vera Cleaver was born in South Dakota; Bill Cleaver in Seattle, Washington. They now pursue their writing as well as their special interests in art, music, and nature, from their home in Lutz, Florida.